MW01087689

F

CONTENTS

LITTLE COMRADE

CHAPTER I

THE THIRTY-FIRST OF JULY

" LET us have coffee on the terrace," Bloem suggested, and, as his companion nodded, lifted a finger to the waiter and gave the order.

Both were a little sad, for this was their last meal together. Though they had known each other less than a fortnight, they had become fast friends. They had been thrown together by chance at the surgical congress at Vienna, where Bloem, finding the American's German lame and halting, had constituted himself a sort of interpreter, and Stewart had reciprocated by polishing away some of the roughnesses and Teutonic involutions of Bloem's formal English.

When the congress ended, they had journeyed back together in leisurely fashion through Germany, spending a day in medieval Nuremberg, another in odorous Würzburg, and a third in mountain-shadowed Heidelberg, where Bloem had sought out some of his old comrades and initiated his American friend into the mysteries of an evening session in the Hirschgasse. Then they had turned northward to Mayence, and so down the terraced Rhine to Cologne. Here they were to part, Bloem to return to his work at Elberfeld, Stewart for a week or two in Brussels and Paris, and then home to America.

Bloem's train was to leave in an hour, and it was the consciousness of this that kept them silent until their waiter came to tell them that their coffee was served. As they followed him through the hall, a tall man in the uniform of a captain of infantry entered from the street. His eyes brightened as he caught sight of Bloem.

"*Ach*, Hermann!" he cried.

Bloem, turning, stopped an instant for a burlesque salute, then threw himself into the other's arms. A moment later, he was dragging him forward to introduce him to Stewart.

"My cousin," he cried, "Ritter Bloem, a soldier as you see—a great fire-eater! Cousin, this is my friend, Dr. Bradford Stewart, whom I had the good fortune to meet at Vienna."

"I am pleased to know you, sir," said the captain, shaking hands and speaking excellent English.

" You must join us," Bloem interposed. " We are just going to have coffee on the terrace. Come," and he caught the other by the arm.

But the captain shook his head.

" No, I cannot come," he said; " really I cannot, much as I should like to do so. Dr. Stewart," he added, a little hesitatingly, " I trust you will not think me discourteous if I take my cousin aside for a moment."

" Certainly not," Stewart assured him.

" I will join you on the terrace," said Bloem, and Stewart, nodding good-by to the captain, followed the waiter, who had stood by during this exchange of greetings, and now led the way to a little table at one corner of the broad balcony looking out over the square.

" Shall I pour the coffee, sir? " he asked, as Stewart sat down.

" No; I will wait for my companion," and, as the waiter bowed and stepped back, Stewart leaned forward with a deep breath of admiration.

Below him lay the green level of the Domhof, its close-clipped trees outlined stiffly against the lights behind them. Beyond rose the choir of the great cathedral, with its fretted pinnacles, and flying buttresses, and towering roof. By day, he had found its exterior somewhat cold and bare and formal, lacking somehow the subtle spirit of true Gothic; but nothing could be more beautiful than it was now, shimmering in the moonlight, bathed in luminous shadow, lace-like and mysterious.

He was still absorbed in this fairy vision when Bloem rejoined him. Even in the half-light of the terrace, Stewart could see that he was deeply moved. His face, usually glowing with healthy color, was almost haggard; his eyes seemed dull and sunken.

"No bad news, I hope?" Stewart asked.

Without answering him, Bloem signaled the waiter to pour the coffee, and sat watching him in silence.

"That will do," he said in German; "we will ring if we have need of you." Then, as the waiter withdrew, he glanced nervously about the terrace. It was deserted save for a noisy group around a table at the farther end. "There is very bad news, my friend," he added, almost in a whisper. "There is going to be—war!"

Stewart stared for an instant, astonished at the gravity of his tone. Then he nodded comprehendingly.

"Yes," he said; "I had not thought of it; but I suppose a war between Austria and Servia *will* affect Germany more or less. Only I was hoping the Powers would interfere and stop it."

"It seems it cannot be stopped," said Bloem, gloomily. "Russia is mobilizing to assist Servia. Austria is Germany's ally, and so Germany must come to her aid. Unless Russia stops her mobilization, we shall declare war against her. Our army has already been called to the colors."

Stewart breathed a little deeper.

"But perhaps Russia will desist when she realizes her danger," he suggested. "She must know she is no match for Germany."

"She does know it," Bloem agreed; "but she also knows that she will not fight alone. It is not against Russia we are mobilizing—it is against France."

"Against France?" echoed the other. "But surely——"

"Do not speak so loud, I beg of you," Bloem cautioned. "What I am telling you is not yet generally known—perhaps the dreadful thing we fear will not happen, after all. But France is Russia's ally—she will be eager for war—for forty years she has been preparing for this moment."

"Yes," agreed Stewart, smiling, "I have heard of '*la revanche*'; I have seen the mourning wreaths on the Strassburg monument. I confess," he added, "that I sympathize with France's dream of regaining her lost provinces. So do most Americans. We are a sentimental people."

"I, too, sympathize with that dream," said Bloem, quickly, "or at least I understand it. So do many Germans. We have come to realize that the seizure of Alsace and Lorraine, however justified by history, was in effect a terrible mistake. We should have been generous in our hour of triumph—that way lay a chance of friendship with a people whose pride remained unbroken by disaster. Instead, we chose to heap insults upon a conquered foe, and we have reaped a merited reward of detestation. Ironically enough, those provinces which cost us so much have been to us a source of weakness, not of strength. We have had to fortify them, to police them, to hold them in stern repression. Even yet, they must be treated as conquered ground. You do not know —you cannot realize—what that means!" He stared out gloomily into the night. "I have served there," he added, hoarsely.

There was something in his tone which sent a shiver across Stewart's scalp, as though he had found himself suddenly at the brink of a horrible abyss into which he dared not turn his eyes. He fancied he could see in his companion's somber face the stirring of ghastly memories, of tragic experience——

"But since France has not yet declared war," he said at last, "surely you will wait——"

"Ah, my friend," Bloem broke in, "we cannot afford to wait. We must strike quickly and with all our strength. There is no secret as to Germany's plan—France must be crushed under a mighty blow before she can defend herself; after that it will be Russia's turn."

"And after that?"

"After that? After that, we shall seize more provinces and exact more huge indemnities—and add just so much to our legacy of fear and hatred! We are bound to a wheel from which we cannot escape."

Stewart looked dazedly out over the lighted square.

"I can't understand it," he said, at last. "I don't understand how such things can be. They aren't possible. They're too terrible to be true. This is a civilized world—such things can never happen—humanity won't endure it!"

Bloem passed a trembling hand before his eyes, as a man awaking from a horrid dream.

"Let us hope so, at least," he said. "But I am afraid; I shake with fear! Europe is topheavy under the burden of her awful armaments; now, or at some future time, she must come tumbling down; she must—she must—" he paused, searching for a word—"she must crumble. Perhaps that time has come."

"I don't believe it," Stewart protested, stoutly. "Some day she will realize the insane folly of this armament, and it will cease."

"I wish I could believe so," said Bloem, sadly; "but you do not know, my friend, how we here in Germany, for example, are weighed down by militarism. You do not know the arrogance, the ignorance, the narrow-mindedness of the military caste. They do nothing for Germany—they add nothing to her art, her science, or her literature—they add nothing to her wealth—they destroy rather than build up—and yet it is they who rule Germany We are a pacific people, we love our homes and a quiet life; we are not a military people, and yet every man in Germany must march to war when the word is given. We ourselves have no voice in the matter. We have only to obey."

"Obey whom?" asked Stewart.

"The Emperor," answered Bloem, bitterly. "With all our progress, my friend, with all our development in science and industry, with all our literature and art, with all our philosophy, we still live in a medieval State, ruled by a king who believes himself divinely appointed, who can do no wrong, and who, in time of war at least, has absolute power over us. And the final decision as to war or peace is wholly in his hands. Understand I do not complain of the Emperor; he has done great things for Germany; he has often cast his influence for peace. But he is surrounded by aristocrats intent only on maintaining their privileges, who are terrified by the growth of democratic ideas; who believe that the only way to checkmate democracy is by a great war. It is they who preach the doctrine of blood and iron; who hold that Cæsar is sacrosanct. The Emperor struggles against them; but some day they will prove too strong for him. Besides, he himself believes in blood and iron; he hates democracy as bitterly as anyone, for it denies the divine right of kings!" He stopped suddenly, his finger to his ear. "Listen!" he said.

Down the street, from the direction of the river, came a low, continuous murmur, as of the wind among the leaves of a forest; then, as it grew clearer, it resolved itself into the tramp, tramp of iron-shod feet. Bloem leaned far forward staring into the darkness; and suddenly, at the corner, three mounted officers appeared; then a line of soldiers wheeled into view; then another and another and another, moving as one man. The head of the column crossed the square, passed behind the church and disappeared, but still the tide poured on with slow and regular undulation, dim, mysterious, and threatening. At last the rear of the column came into view, passed, disappeared; the clatter of iron on stone softened to a shuffle, to a murmur, died away.

With a long breath, Bloem sat erect and passed his handkerchief across his shining forehead.

"There is one battalion," he said; "one unit composed of a thousand lesser units—each unit a man with a soul like yours and mine; with hopes and ambitions; with women to love him; and now marching to death, perhaps, in the ranks yonder without in the least knowing why. There are four million such units in the army the Emperor can call into the field. I am one of them—I shall march like the rest!"

"You!"

"Yes—I am a private in the Elberfeld battalion."

He spread out his delicate, sensitive, surgeon's hands and looked at them. "I was at one time a sergeant," he added, "but my discipline did not satisfy my lieutenant and I was reduced to the ranks."

Stewart also stared at those beautiful hands, so expressive, so expert. How vividly they typified the waste of war!

"But it's absurd," he protested, "that a man like you—highly-trained, highly-educated, a specialist—should be made to shoulder a rifle. In the ranks, you are worth no more than the most ignorant peasant."

"Not so much," corrected Bloem. "Our ideal soldier is one whose obedience is instant and unquestioning."

"But why are you not placed where you would be most efficient—in the hospital corps, perhaps?"

"There are enough old and middle-aged surgeons for that duty. Young men must fight! Besides, I am suspected of having too many ideas!"

He sat for a moment longer staring down at his hands—staring too, perhaps, at his career so ruthlessly shattered—then he shook himself together and glanced across at his companion with a wry little smile.

"You will think me a great croaker!" he said. "It was the first shock—the thought of everything going to pieces. In a day or two, I shall be marching as light-heartedly as all the others—knowing only that I am fighting the enemies of my country— and wishing to know no more!"

But Stewart did not answer the smile. Confused thoughts were flying through his head—thoughts which he struggled to compose into some order or sequence.

Bloem looked at him for a moment, and his smile grew more ironic.

"I can guess what is in your mind," he said. "You are wondering why we march at all—why we offer ourselves as cannon-fodder, if we do not wish to do so. You are thinking of defiances, of revolutions. But there will never be a revolution in Germany—not in this generation."

"Yes, I was thinking something like that," Stewart agreed. "Why will there be no revolution?"

"Because we are too thoroughly drilled in the habit of obedience. That habit is grooved deep into our brains. Were any of us so rash as to start a revolution, the government could stop it with a single word."

"A single word?"

"Yes—'verboten'!" retorted Bloem, with a

short laugh. Then he pushed back his chair and rose abruptly. "I must say good-by. My orders are awaiting me at Elberfeld."

Stewart rose too, his face still mazed with incredulity.

"You really mean——"

"I mean," Bloem broke in, "that to-morrow I go to my depot, hang about my neck the metal tag stamped with my number, put on my uniform and shoulder my rifle. I cease to be an individual—I become a soldier. Good-by, my friend," he added, his voice softening. "Think of me sometimes, in that far-off, sublime America of yours. One thing more —do not linger in Germany—things will be very different here under martial law. Get home as quickly as you can; and, in the midst of your peace and happiness, pity us poor blind worms who are forced to slay each other!"

"But I will go with you to the station," Stewart protested.

"No, no," said Bloem; "you must not do that. I am to meet my cousin. Good-by. *Lebe wohl!*"

"Good-by—and good luck!" and Stewart wrung the hand thrust into his. "You have been most kind to me."

Bloem answered only with a little shake of the

head; then turned resolutely and hastened from the terrace.

Stewart sank back into his seat more moved than he would have believed possible by this parting from a man whom, a fortnight before, he had not known at all. Poor Bloem! To what fate was he being hurried! A cultured man graded down to the level of the hind; a gentleman set to the task of slaughter; a democrat driven to fight in defense of the divine right of kings! But could such a fight succeed? Was any power strong enough to drag back the hands of time——

And then Stewart started violently, for someone had touched him on the shoulder. He looked up to find standing over him a tall man in dark blue uniform and wearing a spiked helmet.

"Your pardon, sir," said the man in careful English; "I am an agent of the police. I must ask you certain questions."

"Very well," agreed Stewart with a smile. "Go ahead—I have nothing to conceal. But won't you sit down?"

"I thank you," and the policeman sat down heavily. "You are, I believe, an American."

"Yes."

"Have you a passport?"

"Yes—I was foolish enough to get one before I left home. All my friends laughed at me and told me I was wasting a dollar!"

"I should like to see it."

Stewart put his hand into an inner pocket, drew out the crackling parchment and passed it over. The other took it, unfolded it, glanced at the red seal and at the date, then read the very vague description of its owner, and finally drew out a notebook.

"Pease sign your name here," he said, and indicated a blank page.

Stewart wrote his name, and the officer compared it with the signature at the bottom of the passport. Then he nodded, folded it up, and handed it back across the table.

"It is quite regular," he said. "For what time have you been in Germany?"

"About two weeks. I attended the surgical congress at Vienna."

"You are a surgeon by profession?"

"Yes."

"You are now on your way home?"

"Yes."

"When will you leave Germany?"

"I am going from here to Aix-la-Chapelle in the

morning, and expect to leave there for Brussels to-morrow afternoon or Sunday morning at the latest."

The officer noted these details in his book.

"At what hotel will you stay in Aachen?" he asked.

"I don't know. Is there a good one near the station?"

"The Kölner Hof is near the station. It is not large, but it is very good. It is starred by Baedeker."

"Then I will go there," said Stewart.

"Very good," and the officer wrote, "Kölner Hof, Aachen," after Stewart's name, closed his note-book and slipped it into his pocket. "You under-stand, sir, that it is our duty to keep watch over all strangers, as much for their own protection as for any other reason."

"Yes," assented Stewart, "I understand. I have heard that there is some danger of war."

"Of that I know nothing," said the other coldly, and rose quickly to his feet. "I bid you good-night, sir."

"Good-night," responded Stewart, and watched the upright figure until it disappeared.

Then, lighting a fresh cigar, he gazed out at the great cathedral, nebulous and dream-like in the darkness, and tried to picture to himself what such a war would mean as Bloem had spoken of. With men by the million dragged into the vast armies, who would harvest Europe's grain, who would work in her factories, who would conduct her business? Above all, who would feed the women and children?

And where would the money come from—the millions needed daily to keep such armies in the field? Where could it come from, save from the sweat of inoffensive people, who must be starved and robbed and ground into the earth until the last penny was wrung from them? Along the line of battle, thousands would meet swift death, and thousands more would struggle back to life through the torments of hell, to find themselves maimed and useless. But how trivial their sufferings beside the slow, hopeless, year-long martyrdom of the countless thousands who would never see a battle, who would know little of the war—who would know only that never thereafter was there food enough, warmth enough——

Stewart started from his reverie to find the waiter putting out the lights. Shivering as with a sudden chill, he hastily sought his room.

CHAPTER II

THE FIRST RUMBLINGS

As Stewart ate his breakfast next morning, he smiled at his absurd fears of the night before. In the clear light of day, Bloem's talk of war seemed mere foolishness. War! Nonsense! Europe would never be guilty of such folly—a deliberate plunge to ruin.

Besides, there were no evidences of war; the life of the city was moving in its accustomed round, so far as Stewart could see; and there was vast reassurance in the quiet and orderly service of the breakfast-room. No doubt the Powers had bethought themselves, had interfered, had stopped the war between Austria and Servia, had ceased mobilization—in a word, had saved Europe from an explosion which would have shaken her from end to end.

But when Stewart asked for his bill, the proprietor, instead of intrusting it as usual to the head-waiter, presented it in person.

"If Herr Stewart would pay in gold, it would be a great favor," he said.

Like all Americans, Stewart, unaccustomed to gold and finding its weight burdensome, carried banknotes whenever it was possible to do so. Emptying his pockets now, he found, besides a miscellaneous lot of silver and nickel and copper, a single small gold coin, value ten marks.

"But I have plenty of paper," he said, and, producing his pocketbook, spread five notes for a hundred marks each before him on the table. "What's the matter with it?"

"There is nothing at all the matter with it, sir," the little fat German hastened to assure him; "only, just at present, there is a preference for gold. I would advise that you get gold for these notes, if possible."

"I have a Cook's letter of credit," said Stewart. "They would give me gold. Where is Cook's office here?"

"It is but a step up the street, sir," answered the other eagerly. "Come, I will show you," and, hastening to the door, he pointed out the office at the end of a row of buildings jutting out toward the cathedral.

Stewart, the banknotes in his hand, hastened

thither, and found quite a crowd of people drawing money on traveler's checks and letters of credit.
He noticed that they were all being paid in gold.
They, too, it seemed, had heard rumors of war, had
been advised to get gold; but most of them treated
the rumors as a joke and were heeding the
advice only because they needed gold to pay their
bills.

Even if there was war, they told each other, it
could not affect them. At most, it would only add
a spice of excitement and adventure to the remainder
of their European tour; what they most feared was
that they would not be permitted to see any of the
fighting! A few of the more timid shamefacedly
confessed that they were getting ready to turn homeward, but by far the greater number proclaimed the
fact that they had made up their minds not to alter
their plans in any detail. So much Stewart gathered as he stood in line waiting his turn; then he
was in front of the cashier's window.

The cashier looked rather dubious when Stewart
laid the banknotes down and asked for gold.

"I am carrying one of your letters of credit,"
Stewart explained, and produced it. "I got these
notes on it at Heidelberg just the other day. Now
it seems they're no good."

"They are perfectly good," the cashier assured him; "but some of the tradespeople, who are always suspicious and ready to take alarm, are demanding gold. How long will you be in Germany?"

"I go to Belgium to-night or to-morrow."

"Then you can use French gold," said the cashier, with visible relief. "Will one hundred marks in German gold carry you through? Yes? I think I can arrange it on that basis;" and when Stewart assented, counted out five twenty-mark pieces and twenty-four twenty-franc pieces. "I think you are wise to leave Germany as soon as possible," he added, in a low tone, as Stewart gathered up this money and bestowed it about his person. "We do not wish to alarm anyone, and we are not offering advice, but if war comes, Germany will not be a pleasant place for strangers."

"Is it really coming?" Stewart asked. "Is there any news?"

"There is nothing definite—just a feeling in the air—but I believe that it is coming," and he turned to the next in line.

Stewart hastened back to the hotel, where his landlord received with reiterated thanks the thirty marks needed to settle the bill. When that transaction

was ended, he glanced nervously about the empty
office, and then leaned close.

"You leave this morning, do you not, sir?" he
asked, in a tone cautiously lowered.

"Yes; I am going to Aix-la-Chapelle."

"Take my advice, sir," said the landlord earnestly, "and do not stop there. Go straight on to
Brussels."

"But why?" asked Stewart. "Everybody is ad-
vising me to get out of Germany. What danger can
there be?"

"No danger, perhaps, but very great annoyance.
It is rumored that the Emperor has already signed
the proclamation declaring Germany in a state of
war. It may be posted at any moment."

"Suppose it is—what then? What difference can
that make to me—or to any American?"

"I see you do not know what those words mean,"
said the little landlord, leaning still closer and speaking with twitching lips. "When Germany is in a
state of war, all civil authority ceases; the military
authority is everywhere supreme. The state takes
charge of all railroads, and no private persons will
be permitted on them until the troops have been
mobilized, which will take at least a week; even
after that, the trains will run only when the military

authorities think proper, and never past the frontier. The telegraphs are taken and will send no private messages; no person may enter or leave the country until his identity is clearly established; every stranger in the country will be placed under arrest, if there is any reason to suspect him. All motor vehicles are seized, all horses, all stores of food. Business stops, because almost all the men must go to the army. I must close my hotel because there will be no men left to work for me. Even if the men were left, there would be no custom when travel ceases. Every shop will be closed which cannot be managed by women; every factory will shut, unless its product is needed by the army. Your letter of credit will be worthless, because there will be no way in which our bankers can get gold from America. No—at that time, Germany will be no place for strangers."

Stewart listened incredulously, for all this sounded like the wildest extravagance. He could not believe that business and industry would fall to pieces like that—it was too firmly founded, too strongly built.

"What I have said is true, sir, believe me," said the little man, earnestly, seeing his skeptical countenance. "One thing more—have you a passport?"

"Yes," said Stewart, and tapped his pocket.

" That is good. That will save you trouble at the
frontier. Ah, here is your baggage. Good-by, sir,
and a safe voyage to your most fortunate country."

A brawny porter shouldered the two suit-cases
which held Stewart's belongings, and the latter followed him along the hall to the door. As he stepped
out upon the terrace, he saw drawn up there about
twenty men—some with the black coats of waiters,
some with the white caps of cooks, some with the
green aprons of porters—while a bearded man in a
spiked helmet was checking off their names in a
little book. At the sound of Stewart's footsteps, he
turned and cast upon him the cold, impersonal
glance of German officialdom. Then he looked at
the porter.

" You will return as quickly as possible," he said
gruffly in German to the latter, and returned to his
checking.

As they crossed the Domhof and skirted the rear
of the cathedral, Stewart noticed that many of the
shops were locked and shuttered, and that the street
seemed strangely deserted. Only as they neared the
station did the crowd increase. It was evident that
many tourists, warned, perhaps, as Stewart had
been, had made up their minds to get out of Germany; but the train drawn up beside the platform

was a long one, and there was room for everybody. It was a good-humored crowd, rather inclined to laugh at its own fears and to protest that this journey was entirely in accordance with a pre-arranged schedule; but it grew quieter and quieter as moment after moment passed and the train did not start.

That a German train should not start precisely on time was certainly unusual; that it should wait for twenty minutes beyond that time was staggering. But the station-master, pacing solemnly up and down the platform, paid no heed to the inquiries addressed to him, and the guards answered only by a shake of the head which might mean anything. Then, quite suddenly, above the noises of the station, menacing and insistent came the low, ceaseless shuffle of approaching feet.

A moment later the head of an infantry column appeared at the station entrance. It halted there, and an officer, in a long, gray cape that fell to his ankles, strode toward the station-master, who hastened to meet him. There was a moment's conference, and then the station-master, saluting for the tenth time, turned to the expectant guards.

"Clear the train!" he shouted in stentorian German, and the guards sprang eagerly to obey.

The scene which followed is quite indescribable.

All the Germans in the train hastened to get off, as did everybody else who understood what was demanded and knew anything of the methods of militarism. But many did not understand; a few who did made the mistake of standing upon what they conceived to be their rights and refusing to be separated from their luggage—and all alike, men, women, and children, were yanked from their seats and deposited upon the platform. Some were deposited upon their feet—but not many. Women screamed as rough and seemingly hostile hands were laid upon them; men, red and inarticulate with anger, attempted ineffectually to resist. In a moment one and all found themselves shut off by a line of police which had suddenly appeared from nowhere and drawn up before the train.

Then a whistle sounded and the soldiers began to file into the carriages in the most systematic manner. Twenty-four men entered each compartment—ten sitting down and fourteen standing up or sitting upon the others' laps. Each coach, therefore, held one hundred and forty-four; and the battalion of seven hundred and twenty men exactly filled five coaches—just as the General Staff had long ago figured that it should.

Stewart, after watching this marvel of organization for a moment, realized that, if any carriages were empty, it would be the ones at the end of the train, and quietly made his way thither. At last, in the rear coach, he came to a compartment in which sat one man, evidently a German, with a melancholy, bearded face. Before the door stood a guard watching the battalion entrain.

" May one get aboard? " Stewart inquired, in his best German.

The guard held up his hand for an instant; then the gold-braided station-master shouted a sentence which Stewart could not distinguish; but the guard dropped his hand and nodded.

Looking back, the American saw a wild mob charging down the platform toward him, and hastily swung himself aboard. As he dropped into his seat, he could hear the shrieks and oaths of the mêlée outside, and the next moment, a party of breathless and disheveled women were storming the door. They were panting, exhausted, inarticulate with rage and chagrin; they fell in, rolled in, stumbled in, until the compartment was jammed.

Stewart, swept from his seat at the first impact, but rallying and doing what he could to bring order out of chaos, could not but admire the manner in which his bearded fellow-passenger clung immov-

ably to his seat until the last woman was aboard,
and then reached quickly out, slammed shut the
door, and held it shut, despite the entreaties of the
lost souls who drifted despairingly past along the
platform, seemingly blind, deaf, and totally unin-
terested in what was passing around him.

Then Stewart looked at the women. Nine were
crowded into the seats; eight were standing; all were
red and perspiring; and most of them had plainly
lost their tempers. Stewart was perspiring himself,
and he got out his handkerchief and mopped his
forehead; then he ventured to speak.

"Well," he said; "so this is war! I have always
heard it was warm work!"

Most of the women merely glared at him and
went on adjusting their clothing, and fastening up
their hair, and straightening their hats; but one, a
buxom woman of forty-eight or fifty, who was
crowded next to him, and who had evidently suffered
more than her share of the general misfortune,
turned sharply.

"Are you an American?" she demanded.

"I am, madam."

"And you stand by and see your countrywomen
treated in this perfectly outrageous fashion?"

"My dear madam," protested Stewart, " what

could one man—even an American—do against a thousand?"

" You could at least———"

" Nonsense, mother," broke in another voice, and Stewart turned to see that it was a slim, pale girl of perhaps twenty-two who spoke. " The gentleman is quite right. Besides, I thought it rather good fun."

" Good fun!" snapped her mother. " Good fun to be jerked about and trampled on and insulted! And where is our baggage? Will we ever see it again?"

" Oh, the baggage is safe enough," Stewart assured her. " The troops will detrain somewhere this side the frontier, and we can all take our old seats."

" But why should they travel by this train? Why should they not take another train? Why should they———"

" Are we all here?" broke in an anxious voice. " Is anyone missing?"

There was a moment's counting, then a general sigh of relief. The number was found correct.

From somewhere up the line a whistle sounded, and the state of the engine-driver's nerves could be

inferred from the jerk with which he started—quite
an American jerk. All the women who were standing, screamed and clutched at each other and swayed
back and forth as if wrestling. Stewart found himself wrestling with the buxom woman.

"I cannot stand!" she declared. "It is outrageous that I should have to stand!" and she fixed
glittering eyes upon the bearded stranger. "No
American would remain seated while a woman of
my age was standing!"

But the bearded stranger gazed blandly out of the
window at the passing landscape.

There was a moment's silence, during which
everyone looked at the heartless culprit. Stewart
had an uneasy feeling that, if he were to do his duty
as an American, he would grab the offender by the
collar and hurl him through the window. Then
the woman next to the stranger bumped resolutely
into him, pressed him into the corner, and disclosed
a few inches of the seat.

"Sit here, Mrs. Field," she said. "We can all
squeeze up a little."

The pressure was tremendous when Mrs. Field
sat down; but the carriage was strongly built and
the sides held. The slender girl came and stood by
Stewart.

"What's it all about?" she asked. "Has there been a riot or something?"

"There is going to be a most awful riot," answered Stewart, "unless all signs fail. Germany is mobilizing her troops to attack France."

"To attack France! How outrageous! It's that Kaiser Wilhelm, I suppose! Well, I hope France will simply clean him up!"

"So do I!" cried her mother. "The Germans are not gentlemen. They do not know how to treat women!"

"'Kochen, Kirche und Kinder!'" quoted somebody, in a high voice.

"But see here," protested Stewart, with a glance at the bearded stranger, who was still staring steadily out of the window, "if I were you, I'd wait till I was out of Germany before saying so. It would be safer!"

"Safer!" echoed an elderly woman with a high nose. "I should like to see them harm an American!"

Stewart turned away to the window with a gesture of despair, and caught the laughing eyes of the girl who stood beside him.

"Don't blame them too much," she said. "They're not themselves. Usually they are all quite polite and well-behaved; but now they are perfectly savage. And I don't blame them. I didn't mind so much, because I'm slim and long-legged and not very dignified; but if I were a stout, elderly woman, rather proud of my appearance, I would bitterly resent being yanked out of a seat and violently propelled across a platform by a bearded ruffian with dirty hands. Wouldn't you?"

"Yes," agreed Stewart, laughing; "I should probably kick and bite and behave in a most undignified manner."

The girl leaned closer.

"Some of them did!" she murmured.

Stewart laughed again and looked at her with fresh interest. It was something to find a woman who could preserve her sense of humor under such circumstances.

"You have been doing the continent?" he asked.

"Yes, seventeen of us; all from Philadelphia."

"And you've had a good time, of course?"

"We'd have had a better if we had brought a man along. I never realized before how valuable men are. Women aren't fitted by nature to wrestle with time-tables and cabbies and hotel-bills and head-waiters. This trip has taught me to respect men more than I have ever done."

" Then it hasn't been wasted. But you say you're from Philadelphia. I know some people in Philadelphia—the Courtlandt Bryces are sort of cousins of mine."

But the girl shook her head.

" That sort of thing happens only in novels," she said. " But there is no reason I shouldn't tell you my name, if you want to know it. It is Millicent Field, and its possessor is very undistinguished— just a school-teacher—not at all in the same social circle as the Courtlandt Bryces."

Stewart colored a little.

" My name is Bradford Stewart," he said, " and I also am very undistinguished—just a surgeon on the staff at Johns Hopkins. Did you get to Vienna? "

" No; that was too far for us."

" There was a clinic there; I saw some wonderful things. These German surgeons certainly know their business."

Miss Field made a little grimace.

" Perhaps," she admitted. " But do you know the impression of Germany that I am taking home with me? It is that Germany is a country run solely in the interests of the male half of creation. Women are tolerated only because they are necessary in the scheme of things."

Stewart laughed.

" There was a book published a year or two ago," he said, " called 'Germany and the Germans.' Perhaps you read it? "

" No."

" I remember it for one remark. Its author says that Germany is the only country on earth where the men's hands are better kept than the women's."

Miss Field clapped her hands in delight.

" Delicious! " she cried. " Splendid! And it is true," she added, more seriously. " Did you see the women cleaning the streets in Munich? "

" Yes."

" And harvesting the grain, and spreading manure, and carrying great burdens—doing all the dirty work and the heavy work. What are the men doing, I should like to know? "

" Madam," spoke up the bearded stranger by the window, in a deep voice which made everybody jump, " I will tell you what the men are doing— they are in the army, preparing themselves for the defense of their fatherland. Do you think it is of choice they leave the harvesting and street-cleaning and carrying of burdens to their mothers and wives

and sisters? No; it is because for them is reserved
a greater task—the task of confronting the revenge-
ful hate of France, the envious hate of England, the
cruel hate of Russia. That is their task to-day,
madam, and they accept it with light hearts, confident of victory!"

There was a moment's silence. Mrs. Field was
the first to find her voice.

" All the same," she said, " that does not justify
the use of cows as draft animals!"

The German stared at her an instant in astonishment, then turned away to the window with a gesture of contempt, as of one who refuses to argue
with lunatics, and paid no further heed to the
Americans.

With them, the conversation turned from war,
which none of them really believed would come, to
home, for which they were all longing. Home,
Stewart told himself, means everything to middle-
aged women of fixed habits. It was astonishing
that they should tear themselves away from it, even
for a tour of Europe, for to them travel meant
martyrdom. Home! How their eyes brightened
as they spoke the word! They were going through
to Brussels, then to Ostend, after a look at Ghent
and Bruges, and so to England and their boat.

"I intend to spend the afternoon at Aix-la-Chapelle," said Stewart, "and go on to Brussels to-night or in the morning. Perhaps I shall see you there."

Miss Field mentioned the hotel at which the party would stop.

"What is there at Aix-la-Chapelle?" she asked. "I suppose I ought to know, but I don't."

"There's a cathedral, with the tomb of Charlemagne, and his throne, and a lot of other relics. I was always impressed by Charlemagne. He was the real thing in the way of emperors."

"I should like to see his tomb," said Miss Field. "Why can't we stop at Aix-la-Chapelle, mother?"

But Mrs, Field shook her head.

"We will get out of Germany as quickly as we can," she said, and the other members of the party nodded their hearty agreement.

Meanwhile the train rolled steadily on through a beautiful and peaceful country, where war seemed incredible and undreamed of. White villas dotted the thickly-wooded hillsides; quaint villages huddled in the valleys. And finally the train crossed a long viaduct and rumbled into the station at Aix-la-Chapelle.

The platform was deserted, save for a few guards

and porters. Stewart opened the door and was about to step out, when a guard waved him violently back. Looking forward, he saw that the soldiers were detraining.

" Good! " he said. " You can get your old seats again! " and, catching the eye of the guard, gave him a nod which promised a liberal tip.

That worthy understood it perfectly, and the moment the last soldier was on the platform, he beckoned to Stewart and his party, assisted them to find their old compartments, ejected a peasant who had taken refuge in one of them, assured the ladies that they would have no further inconvenience, and summoned a porter to take charge of Stewart's suitcases. In short, he did everything he could to earn the shining three-mark piece which Stewart slipped into his hand.

And then, after receiving the thanks of the ladies and promising to look them up in Brussels, Stewart followed his porter across the platform to the entrance.

Millicent Field looked after him a little wistfully.

" How easy it is for a man to do things! " she remarked to nobody in particular. " Never speak to me again of woman suffrage! "

CHAPTER III

" STATE OF WAR "

STEWART, following his porter, was engulfed in the human tide which had been beating clamorously against the gates, and which surged forward across the platform as soon as they were opened. There were tourists of all nations, alarmed by the threat of war, and there were also many people who, to Stewart at least, appeared to be Germans; and all of them were running toward the train, looking neither to the right nor left, dragging along as much luggage as they could carry.

As he stepped aside for a moment out of the way of this torrent, Stewart found himself beside the bearded stranger who had waxed eloquent in defense of Germany. He was watching the crowd with a look at once mocking and sardonic, as a spider might watch a fly struggling vainly to escape from the web. He glanced at Stewart, then turned away without any sign of recognition.

" Where do you go, sir? " the porter asked, when they were safely through the gates.

" To the Kölner Hof."

" It is but a step," said the porter, and he un-hooked his belt, passed it through the handles of the suit-cases, hooked it together again and lifted it to his shoulder. " This way, sir, if you please."

The Kölner Hof proved to be a modest inn just around the corner, where Stewart was received most cordially by the plump, high-colored landlady. Lunch would be ready in a few minutes; mean-while, if the gentleman would follow the waiter, he would be shown to a room where he could remove the traces of his journey. But first would the gen-tleman fill in the blank required by the police?

So Stewart filled in the blank, which demanded his name, his nationality, his age, his business, his home address, the place from which he had come to Aix-la-Chapelle and the place to which he would go on leaving it, handed it back to the smiling landlady, and followed an ugly, hang-dog waiter up the stair.

The room into which he was shown was a very pleasant one, scrupulously clean, and as he made his toilet, Stewart reflected how much more of comfort and how much warmer welcome was often to be had at the small inns than at the big ones, and mentally thanked the officer of police who had recommended this one. He found he had further reason for gratitude when he sat down to lunch, served on a little table set in one corner of a shady court—the best lunch he had eaten for a long time, as he told the landlady when she came out presently, knitting in hand, and sat down near him. She could speak a little English, it appeared, and a little French, and these, with Stewart's little German, afforded a medium of communication limping, it is true, but sufficient.

She received the compliments of her guest with the dignity of one who knew them to be deserved.

" I do what I can to please my patrons," she said; " and indeed I have had no cause to complain, for the season has been very good. But this war—it will ruin us innkeepers—there will be no more travelers. Already, I hear, Spa, Ostend, Carlsbad, Baden—such places as those—are deserted just when the season should be at its best. What do you think of it—this war? "

" Most probably it is just another scare," said Stewart. " War seems scarcely possible in these days—it is too cruel, too absurd. An agreement will be reached."

" I am sure I hope so, sir; but it looks very bad. For three days now our troops have been passing through Aachen toward the frontier."

"How far away is the frontier?"

"About ten miles. The customhouse is at Herbesthal."

"Ten miles!" echoed Stewart in surprise. "The frontier of France?"

"Oh, no—the frontier of Belgium."

"But why should they concentrate along the Belgian frontier?" Stewart demanded.

"Perhaps they fear an attack from that direction. Or perhaps," she added, calmly, "they are preparing to seize Belgium. I have often heard it said that Belgium should belong to Germany."

"But look here," protested Stewart, hotly, "Germany can't seize a country just because it happens to be smaller and weaker than she is!"

"Can't she?" inquired the landlady, seemingly astonished at his indignation. "Why is that?"

Her eyes were shining strangely as she lowered them to her knitting; and there was a moment's silence, broken only by the rapid clicking of her needles. For Stewart found himself unable to answer her question. Ever since history began, big countries had been seizing smaller ones, and great powers crushing weaker ones. If Austria might seize Bosnia and Italy Tripoli, why might not Germany seize Belgium? And he suddenly realized that, in spite of protests and denials and hypocrisies, between nation and nation the law of the jungle was, even yet, often the only law!

"At any rate," pursued the landlady, at last, "I have heard that great intrenchments are being built all along there, and that supplies for a million men have been assembled. There has been talk of war many times before, and nothing has come of it; but there have never been such preparations as these."

"Let us hope it is only the Kaiser rattling his sword again—a little louder than usual. I confess," he added more soberly, "that as an American I haven't much sympathy with Prussian militarism. I have sometimes thought that a war which would put an end to it once for all would be a good thing."

The woman shot him a glance surprisingly quick and piercing.

"That is also the opinion of many here in Germany," she said in a low voice; "but it is an opinion which cannot be uttered." She checked herself quickly as the ugly waiter approached. "How long will the gentleman remain in Aachen?" she asked, in another tone.

"I am going on to Brussels this evening. There is a train at six o'clock, is there not?"

"At six o'clock, yes, sir. It will be well for the gentleman to have a light dinner before his departure. The train may be delayed—and the journey to Brussels is of seven hours."

"Very well," agreed Stewart, rising. "I will be back about five. How does one get to the cathedral?"

"Turn to your right, sir, as you leave the hotel. The first street is the Franzstrasse. It will lead you straight to the church."

Stewart thanked her and set off. The Franzstrasse proved to be a wide thoroughfare, bordered by handsome shops, but many of them were closed and the street itself was almost deserted. It opened upon a narrower street, at the end of which Stewart could see the lofty choir of the minster.

Presently he became aware of a chorus of high-pitched voices, which grew more and more distinct as he advanced. It sounded like a lot of women in violent altercation, and then in a moment he saw what it was, for he came out upon an open square covered with market-stalls, and so crowded that one could scarcely get across it. Plainly the frugal wives of Aachen were laying in supplies against the time when all food would grow scarce and dear, and from the din of high-pitched bargaining it was

evident that the crafty market-people had already
begun to advance their prices.

Stewart paused for a while to contemplate this
scene, far more violent and war-like than any he
had yet witnessed; then, edging around the crowd,
he arrived at the cathedral, the most irregular and
eccentric that he had ever seen—a towering Gothic
choir attached to an octagonal Byzantine nave. But
that nave is very impressive, as Stewart found when
he stepped inside it; and then, on a block of stone
in its pavement, he saw the words, " Carlo Magno,"
and knew that he was at the tomb of the great Emperor.

It is perhaps not really the tomb, but for emo-
tional purposes it answers very well, and there can
be no question about the marble throne and other
relics which Stewart presently inspected, under the
guidance of a black-clad verger. Then, as there
was a service in progress in the choir, he sat down,
at the verger's suggestion, to wait till it was
over.

In a small chapel at his right, a group of candles
glowed before an altar dedicated to the Virgin, and
here, on the low benches, many women knelt in
prayer. More and more slipped in quietly—young
women, old women, some shabby, some well-clad—

until the benches were full; and after that the new-
comers knelt on the stone pavement and besought the
Mother of Christ to guard their sons and husbands
and sweethearts, summoned to fight the battles of
the Emperor. Looking at them—at their bowed
heads, their drawn faces, their shrinking figures—
Stewart realized for the first time how terrible is
the burden which war lays on women. To bear
sons, to rear them—only to see them march away
when the dreadful summons came; to bid good-by
to husband or to lover, crushing back the tears,
masking the stricken heart; and then to wait, day
after dreary day, in agony at every rumor, at every
knock, at every passing footstep, with no refuge
save in prayer——

But such thoughts were too painful. To distract
them, he got out his Baedeker and turned its pages
absently until he came to Aachen. First the railway
stations—there were four, it seemed; then the hotels
—the Grand Monarque, the Nuellens, the Hôtel de
l'Empereur, the du Nord—strange that so many of
them should be French, in name at least!—the
Monopol, the Imperial Crown—but where was the
Kölner Hof? He ran through the list again more
carefully—no, it was not there. And yet that police-
officer at Cologne had asserted not only that it was

in Baedeker, but that it was honored with a star!
Perhaps in the German edition——

A touch on the arm apprised him that the verger
was ready to take him through the choir, where the
service was ended, and Stewart slipped his book back
into his pocket and followed him. It is a lovely
choir, soaring toward the heavens in airy beauty, but
Stewart had no eyes for it. He found suddenly that
he wanted to get away. He was vaguely uneasy.
The memory of those kneeling women weighed him
down. For the first time he really believed that war
might come.

So he tipped the verger and left the church and
came out into the streets again, to find them emp-
tier than ever. Nearly all the shops were closed;
there was no vehicle of any kind; there were scarcely
any people. And then, as he turned the corner into
the wide square in front of the town-hall, he saw
where at least some of the people were, for a great
crowd had gathered there—a crowd of women and
children and old men—while from the steps before
the entrance an official in gold-laced uniform and
cocked hat was delivering a harangue.

At first, Stewart could catch only a word here and
there, but as he edged closer, he found that the
speech was a eulogy of the Kaiser—of his high wis-

dom, his supreme greatness, his passionate love for his people. The Kaiser had not sought war, he had strained every nerve for peace; but the jealous enemies who ringed Germany round, who looked with envy upon her greatness and dreamed only of destroying her, would not give her peace. So, with firm heart and abiding trust in God, the Emperor had donned his shining armor and unsheathed his sword, confident that Germany would emerge from the struggle greater and stronger than ever.

Then the speaker read the Emperor's address, and reminded his hearers that all they possessed, even to their lives and the lives of their loved ones, belonged to their Fatherland, to be yielded ungrudgingly when need arose. He cautioned them that the military power was now supreme, not to be questioned. It would brook no resistance nor interference. Disobedience would be severely dealt with. It was for each of them to go quietly about his affairs, trusting in the Emperor's wisdom, and to pray for victory.

There were some scattered cheers, but the crowd for the most part stood in dazed silence and watched two men put up beside the entrance to the rathhaus the proclamation which declared Germany in a state of war. Down the furrowed cheeks of many of the

older people the hot tears poured in streams, perhaps
at remembrance of the horrors and suffering of Germany's last war with France, and some partial real-
ization that far greater horrors and suffering were
to come. Then by twos and threes they drifted
away to their homes, talking in bated undertone, or
shuffling silently along, staring straight before them.
In every face were fear and grief and a sullen questioning of fate.

Why had this horror been decreed for them?
What had they done that this terrible burden should
be laid upon them? What could war bring any one
of them but sorrow and privation? Was there no
way of escape? Had they no voice in their own
destiny? These were the questions which surged
through Stewart's mind as he slowly crossed the
square and made his way along the silent streets
back toward his hotel. At almost every corner a
red poster stared at him—a poster bearing the Prussian eagle and the Kaiser's name. " The sword has
been thrust into our hands," the Kaiser wrote. " We
must defend our Fatherland and our homes against
the assaults of our enemies. Forward with God,
who will be with us, as He was with our fathers!"

Sad as he had never been before, Stewart walked
on. Something was desperately wrong somewhere;

this people did not want war—most probably even the Kaiser did not want war. Yet war had come; the fate of Europe was trembling in the balance; millions of men were being driven to a detested task. Caught up in mighty armies by a force there was no resisting, they were marching blindly to kill and be killed——

A sudden outbreak of angry voices in the street ahead startled Stewart from his thoughts. A section of soldiers was halted before a house at whose door a violent controversy was in progress between their sergeant and a wrinkled old woman.

" I tell you we must have him," the sergeant shouted, as though for the twentieth time.

" And I tell you his wife is dying," shrieked the woman. " He has permission from his captain."

" I know nothing about that. My orders are to gather in all stragglers."

" It is only a question of a few hours."

" He must come now," repeated the sergeant, doggedly. " Those are the orders. If he disobeys them—if I am compelled to use force—he will be treated as a deserter. Will you tell him, or must I send my men in to get him? "

The sunken eyes flamed with rage, the wrinkled face was contorted with hate—but only for an in-

stant. The flame died; old age, despair, the habit
of obedience, reasserted themselves. A tear trickled
down the cheek—a tear of helplessness and resigna-
tion.

"I will tell him, sir," she said, and disappeared
indoors.

The sergeant turned back to his men, cursing horribly to himself. Suddenly he spat upon the pavement in disgust.

"A devil's job!" he muttered, and took a short
turn up and down, without looking at his men. In
a moment the old woman reappeared in the door.
"Well, mother?" he demanded, gruffly.

"I have told him. He will be here at once."

As she spoke, a fair-haired youth of perhaps
twenty appeared on the threshold and saluted. His
eyes were red with weeping, but he held himself
proudly erect.

"Hermann Gronau?" asked the sergeant.

"Yes."

"Fall in!"

With a shriek of anguish, the woman threw her
arms about him and strained him close.

"My boy!" she moaned. "My youngest one—
my baby—they are taking you also!"

"I shall be back, mother, never fear," he said, and

loosened her arms gently. "You will write me when—when it is over."

"Yes," she promised, and he took his place in the ranks.

"March!" cried the sergeant, and the section tramped away with Gronau in its midst. At the corner, he turned and waved his hand in farewell to the old woman. For a moment longer she stood clutching at the door and staring at the place where he had vanished, then turned slowly back into the house.

CHAPTER IV

THE MYSTERY OF THE SATIN SLIPPERS

STEWART, awakening from the contemplation of this poignant drama—one of thousands such enacting at that moment all over Europe—realized that he was lingering unduly and hastened his steps. At the end of five minutes, he was again in the wide Franz-strasse, and, turning the last corner, saw his land-lady standing at her door, looking anxiously up and down the street.

Her face brightened with relief when she saw him —a relief so evidently deep and genuine that Stewart was a little puzzled by it.

"But I am glad to see you!" she cried as he came up, her face wreathed in smiles. "I was imagining the most horrible things. I feared I know not what! But you are safe, it seems."

"Quite safe. In fact, I was never in any danger."

"I was foolish, no doubt, to have fear. But in times like these, one never knows what may happen."

"True enough," Stewart agreed. "Still, an American with a passport in his pocket ought to be safe anywhere."

"Ah; you have a passport—that is good. That will simplify matters. The police have been here to question you. They will return presently."

"The police?"

"There have been some spies captured, it seems. And there are many who are trying to leave the country. So everyone is suspected. You are not German-born, I hope? If you were, I fear not even your passport would be of use."

They had walked back together along the hall as they talked, and now stopped at the foot of the stair. The landlady seemed very nervous—as was perhaps natural amid the alarms of war. She scarcely listened to his assurance that he was American by birth. Little beads of perspiration stood out across her forehead——

"The police visited your room," she rattled on. "You will perhaps find your baggage disarranged."

Stewart smiled wryly.

"So it seems they really suspect me?"

"They suspect everyone," the landlady repeated.

She was standing with her back toward the door, and Stewart wondered why she should watch his face so closely.

Suddenly, over her shoulder, he saw the ugly waiter with the hang-dog air approaching along the hall.

"Such anxiety is quite natural," said the landlady rapidly in German, raising her voice a little. "I can understand it. But it is not remarkable that you should have missed her—the trains are so irregular. I will send her to you the moment she arrives. Ah, Hans," she added, turning at the sound of the waiter's footsteps, "so you are back at last! You will take up some hot water to the gentleman at once. And now you will excuse me, sir; I have the dinner to attend to," and she hurried away, carrying the waiter with her.

Stewart stood for an instant staring after her; then he turned and mounted slowly to his room. But what had the woman meant? Why should he be anxious? Who was it he had missed? "I will send her to you the moment she arrives." No—she could not have said that—it was impossible that she should have said that. He must have misunderstood; his German was very second-rate, and she had spoken rapidly. But what *had* she said?

He was still pondering this problem, when a
knock at the door told him that the hot water had
arrived. As he opened the door, the landlady's voice
came shrilly up the stair.

"Hans!" she called. "There is something wrong
with the stove. Hasten! Hasten!"

Stewart took the can which was thrust hastily
into his hand, turned back into the room, and proceeded to make a leisurely toilet. If the landlady
had not told him, he would never have suspected
that his baggage had been searched by the police,
for everything seemed to be where he had left it.
But then he was a hasty and careless packer, by no
means precise——

That vague feeling of uneasiness which had
shaken him in the church swept over him again,
stronger than before; there was something wrong
somewhere; the meshes of an invisible net seemed
closing about him. More than once he caught himself standing quite still, in an attitude of profound
meditation, though he was not conscious that he had
really been thinking of anything. Evidently the
events of the day had shaken him more deeply
than he had realized.

"Come, old man," he said at last, "this won't
do. Pull yourself together."

And then a sudden vivid memory rose before him of those praying women, of that wrinkled mother gazing despairingly after her youngest born as he was marched away perhaps forever, of the set faces of the crowd shuffling silently homeward——

He had been absently turning over the contents of one of his bags, searching for a necktie, when he found himself staring at a pair of satin ball-slippers, into each of which was stuffed a blue silk stocking. For quite a minute he stared, doubting his own senses; then he picked up one of the slippers and looked at it.

It was a tiny affair, very delicate and beautiful—a real jewel in footwear, such as Stewart, with his limited feminine experience, had never seen before. Indeed, he might have doubted that they were intended for actual service, but for the slight discoloration inside the heel, which proved that these had been worn more than once. Very deliberately he drew out the stocking, also a jewel in its way, of a texture so diaphanous as to be almost cobweblike. Then he picked up the other slipper and held them side by side. Yes, they were mates——

"But where on earth could I have picked them up?" he asked himself. "In what strange fit of absent-mindedness could I have packed them with

my things? But I couldn't have picked them up—
I never saw them before——"

He sat down suddenly, a slipper in either hand.
They must have come from somewhere—they could
not have concealed themselves among his things.
If he had not placed them there, then someone else
had. But who? And for what purpose? The
police? His landlady had said that they had
searched his luggage; but what possible object could
they have had for increasing it by two satin slippers and a pair of stockings? Such an action was
farcical—French-farcical!—but he could not be in-
criminated in such a way. He had no wife to be
made jealous! And even if he had——

"This is the last straw!" he muttered to himself. "Either the world has gone mad, or I
have."

Moving as in a dream, he placed the slippers side
by side upon the floor, contemplated them for a moment longer, and then proceeded slowly with his
dressing. He found an unaccustomed difficulty in
putting his buttons in his cuffs, and then he remembered that it was a tie he had been looking for when
he found the slippers. The slippers! He turned
and glanced at them. Yes—they were still there—
they had not vanished. Very coquettish they

appeared, standing there side by side, as though waiting for their owner.

And suddenly Stewart smiled a crooked smile.

"Only one thing is necessary to complete this pantomime," he told himself, "and that is that the Princess should suddenly appear and claim them. Well, I'm willing! A woman with a foot like that——"

There was a knock at the door.

"In a moment!" he called.

"But it is I!" cried a woman's voice in English—a sweet, high-pitched voice, quivering with excitement. "It is I!" and the door was flung open with a crash.

A woman rushed toward him—he saw vaguely her vivid face, her shining eyes; behind her, more vaguely still, he saw the staring eyes of the hang-dog waiter. Then she was upon him.

"At last!" she cried, and flung her arms about him and kissed him on the lips—kissed him closely, passionately, as he had never been kissed before.

CHAPTER V.

ONE WAY TO ACQUIRE A WIFE

STEWART, standing petrified, collar in hand, thrilling with the warmth of that caress, was conscious that his free arm had dropped about the woman's waist, and that she was cuddling to him, patting him excitedly on the cheek and smiling up into his eyes. Then, over her shoulder, he caught a glimpse of the sardonic smile on the ugly face of the waiter as he withdrew and closed the door.

"But how glad I am!" the woman rattled on, at the top of her voice. "And what a journey! I am covered with dirt! I shall need gallons of water!"

She walked rapidly to the door, opened it, and looked out. Then she closed and locked it, and, to his amazement, caught up one of his handkerchiefs and hung it over the knob so that it masked the keyhole.

"They will not suspect," she said, in a lower tone, noticing his look. "They will suppose it is to conceal our marital endearments! Now we can talk. But we will keep to English, if you do not mind. Someone might pass. Is everything arranged? Is the passport in order?"

Her eyes were shining with excitement, her lips were trembling. As he still stood staring, she came close to him and shook his arm.

"Can it be that you do not know English?" she demanded. "But that would be too stupid! You understand English, do you not?"

"Yes, madam," stammered Stewart. "At least, I have always thought so."

"Then why do you not answer? Is anything wrong? You look as though you did not expect me."

"Madam," answered Stewart, gravely, "will you kindly pinch me on the arm—here in the tender part? I have been told that is a test."

She nipped him with a violence that made him jump.

"Do not tell me that you are drunk!" she hissed, viciously. "That would be too much! Drunk at such a moment!"

But Stewart had begun to pull himself together.

"No, madam, I am not drunk," he assured her; "and your pinch convinces me that I am not dreaming." He rubbed his arm thoughtfully. "There remains only one hypothesis—that I have suddenly gone mad. And yet I have never heard of any madness in my family, nor until this moment detected any symptoms in myself."

" Is this a time for fooling? " she snapped. " Tell me at once——"

" There is, of course, another hypothesis," went on Stewart, calmly, " and that is that it is you who are mad——"

" Were you not expecting me? " she repeated.

Stewart's eyes fell upon the satin slippers, and he smiled.

" Why, certainly I was expecting you," he answered. " I was just saying to myself that the only thing lacking in this fairy-tale was the beautiful Cinderella—and presto; there you were! "

She looked at him wildly, her eyes dark with fear. Suddenly she caught her lower lip between the thumb and little finger of her left hand, and stood a moment expectantly, holding it so and staring up at him. Then, as he stared back uncomprehendingly, she dropped into a chair and burst into a flood of tears.

Now a pretty woman in tears is, as everyone knows, a sight to melt a heart of stone, especially if that heart be masculine. This woman was extremely pretty, and Stewart's heart was very masculine, with nothing granitic about it.

"Oh, come," he protested, "it can't be so bad as that! Let us sit down and talk this thing out quietly. Evidently there is a mistake somewhere."

"Then you did not expect me?" she demanded, mopping her eyes.

"Expect you? No—except as the fulfillment of a fairy-tale."

"You do not know who I am?"

"I haven't the slightest idea."

"Nor why I am here?"

"No."

"*Ah, ciel!*" she breathed, "then I am lost!" and she turned so pale that Stewart thought she was going to faint.

"Lost!" he protested. "In what way lost? What do you mean?"

By a mighty effort she fought back the faintness and regained a little of her self-control.

"At this hotel," she explained, in a hoarse voice, "I was to have met a man who was to accompany me across the frontier. He had a passport for both of us—for himself and for his wife."

"You were to pass as his wife?"

"Yes."

" But you did not know the man? "

" Evidently—or I should not have——"

She stopped, her face crimson with embarrassment.

" H-m! " said Stewart, reflecting that he, at least, had no reason to regret the mistake. " Perhaps this unknown is in some other room."

" No; you are the only person in the hotel."

" Evidently, then, he has not arrived."

" Evidently," she assented, and stared moodily at the floor, twisting her handkerchief in nervous, trembling hands.

Stewart rubbed his chin thoughtfully as he looked at her. She seemed not more than twenty, and she was almost startlingly beautiful, with that peculiar lustrous duskiness of skin more common among the Latin races than with us. Slightly built, she yet gave the impression of having in reserve unusual nervous energy, which would brace her to meet any crisis.

But what was she doing here? Why should she be driven to leave Germany as the wife of a man whom she had never seen? Or was it all a lie— was she merely an adventuress seeking a fresh victim?

Stewart looked at her again, then he put that

thought away, definitely and forever. He had had enough experience of women, as surgeon in a public clinic, to tell innocence from vice; and he knew that it was innocence he was facing now.

" You say you can't leave Germany without a passport? " he asked at last.

" No one can leave Germany without a passport." She sat up suddenly and looked at him, a new light in her eyes. " Is it possible," she demanded, with trembling lips, " can it be possible that you possess a passport? "

" Why, yes," said Stewart, " I have a passport. Unfortunately, it is for myself alone. Never having had a wife——"

But she was standing before him, her hands outstretched, tremulous with eagerness.

" Let me see it! " she cried. " Oh, let me see it! "

He got it out, gave it to her, and watched her as she unfolded it. Here was a woman, he told himself, such as he had never met before—a woman of verve, of fire——

She was looking up at him with flaming eyes.

" Mr. Stewart," she said, in a low voice, " you can save me, if you will."

" Save you? " echoed Stewart. " But how? "

She held the open passport toward him.

"See, here, just below your name, there is a blank space covered with little parallel lines. If you will permit me to write in that space the words 'accompanied by his wife,' I am saved. The passport will then be for both of us."

"Or would be," agreed Stewart, dryly, "if you were my wife. As it happens, you are not!"

"It is such a little thing I ask of you," she pleaded. "We go to the station together—we take our seats in the train—at the frontier you show your passport. An hour later we shall be at Liège, and there our ways will part; but you will have done a noble action."

There was witchery in her eyes, in her voice. Stewart felt himself slipping—slipping; but he caught himself in time.

"I am afraid," he said, gently, "that you will have to tell me first what it is all about."

"I can tell you in a word," she answered, drawing very near to him, and speaking almost in a whisper. "I am a Frenchwoman."

"But surely," Stewart protested, "the Germans will not prevent your return to France! Why should they do that?"

"It is not a question of returning, but of escaping. I am an Alsatian. I was born at Strassburg."

"Oh," said Stewart, remembering the tone in which Bloem had spoken of Alsace-Lorraine and beginning vaguely to understand. "An Alsatian."

"Yes; but only Alsatians understand the meaning of that word. To be an Alsatian is to be a slave, is to be the victim of insult, oppression, tyranny past all belief. My father was murdered by the Germans; my two brothers have been dragged away into the German army and sent to fight the Russians, since Germany knows well that no Alsatian corps would fight the French! Oh, how we have prayed and prayed for this war of restitution—the war which will give us back to France!"

"Yes; I hope it will," agreed Stewart, heartily.

"Of a certainty you do!" she said, eagerly. "All Americans do. Not one have I ever known who took the German side. How could they? How could any American be on the side of despotism? Oh, impossible! America is on our side! And you, as an American, will assist me to escape my enemies."

"Your enemies?"

"I will not deceive you," she said, earnestly. "I trust you. I have lived all my life at Strassburg and at Metz, those two outposts against France—those two great fortresses of cities which the Germans have done their utmost to make impregnable, but which are not impregnable if attacked in a certain way. They have their weak spot, just as every fortress has. I have dissembled, I have lied—I have pretended to admire the gold-laced pigs—I have permitted them to kiss my hand—I have listened to their confidences, their hopes and fears—I have even joined in their toast 'The Day!' Always, always have I kept my eyes and ears open. Bit by bit, have I gathered what I sought—a hint here, a hint there . . . I must get to France, my friend, and you must help me! Surely you will be glad to strike a blow at these braggart Prussians! It is not for myself I ask it—though, if I am taken, there will be for me only one brief moment, facing a file of soldiers; I ask it for France—for your sister Republic!"

If it had been for France alone, Stewart might still have hesitated; but as he gazed down into that eloquent face, wrung with desperate anxiety, he seemed to see, as in a vision, a file of soldiers in spiked helmets facing a wall where stood a lovely girl, her eyes flaming, her head flung back, smiling contemptuously at the leveled rifles; he saw again the flickering candles at the Virgin's feet——

"Very well," he said, abruptly—almost harshly. "I consent."

Before he could draw back, she had flung herself on her knees before him, had caught his hand, and was covering it with tears and kisses.

"Come, come, my dear," he said. "That won't do!" And he bent over her and raised her to her feet.

She was shaken with great sobs, and as she turned her streaming eyes up to him, her lips moving as if in prayer, Stewart saw how young she was, how lonely, how beautiful, how greatly in need of help. She had been fighting for her country with all her strength, with every resource, desperately, every nerve a-strain—and victory had been too much for her. But in a moment she had back her self-control.

"There, it is finished!" she said, smiling through her tears. "But the joy of your words was almost too great. I shall not behave like that again. And I shall not try to thank you. I think you understand—I cannot thank you—there are no words great enough."

Stewart nodded, smilingly.

"Yes; I understand," he said.

"We have many things to do," she went on, rapidly, passing her handkerchief across her eyes with the gesture of one who puts sentiment aside.

"First, the passport," and she caught it up from the chair on which she had laid it.

"I would point out to you," said Stewart, "that there may be a certain danger in adding the words you mentioned."

"But it is precisely for those words this blank space has been left."

"That may be true; but unless your handwriting is identical with that on the rest of the passport, and the ink the same, the first person who looks at it will detect the forgery."

"Trust me," she said, and drawing a chair to the table, laid the passport before her and studied it carefully. From the little bag she had carried on her arm, she took a fountain-pen. She tested it on her finger-nail, and then, easily and rapidly, wrote "accompanied by his wife" across the blank space below Stewart's name.

Stewart, staring down over her shoulder, was astonished by the cleverness of the forgery. It was perfect.

"There," she added, "let it lie for five minutes and no one on earth can tell that those words were not written at the same time and by the same hand as all the others."

A sudden doubt shook her hearer. Where had she

learned to forge like that? Perhaps, after all——

She read his thought in his eyes.

" To imitate handwriting is something which every member of the secret service must learn to do. This, on your passport, is a formal hand very easily imitated. But I must rid myself of this pen."

She glanced quickly about the room, went to the open fireplace and threw the pen above the bricks which closed it off from the flue. Then she came back, motioned him to sit down, and drew a chair very close to his.

" Now we have certain details to arrange," she said. " Your name is Bradford Stewart? "

" Yes."

" Have you a sobriquet? "

" A what? "

" A name of familiarity," she explained, " used only by your family or your friends."

" Oh, a nickname! Well," he admitted, unwillingly, " my father always called me Tommy."

" Tommy! Excellent! I shall call you Tommy!"

" But I detest Tommy," he objected.

" No matter!" she said, peremptorily. " It will have to do. What is your profession? "

" I am a surgeon."

"Where do you live in America?"

"At Baltimore, in the State of Maryland."

"Where have you been in Europe?"

"To a clinical congress at Vienna, and then back through Germany."

"Perfect! It could not be better! Now, listen most carefully. The name of your wife is Mary. You have been married four years."

"Any children?" asked Stewart.

"Please be serious!" she protested, but from the sparkle in her eye Stewart saw that she was not offended.

"I should have liked a boy of three and a girl of two," he explained. "But no matter—go ahead."

"While you went to Vienna to attend your horrible clinic and learn new ways of cutting up human bodies, your wife remained at Spa, because of a slight nervous affection——"

"From which," said Stewart, "I am happy to see that she has entirely recovered."

"Yes," she agreed; "she is quite well again. Spa is in Belgium, so the Germans cannot disprove the story. We arranged to meet here and to go on to Brussels together. Do you understand?"

"Perfectly," said Stewart, who was thoroughly enjoying himself. "By the way, Mary," he added,

" no doubt it was your shoes and stockings I found in my grip awhile ago," and he pointed to where the slippers stood side by side.

His companion stared at them for an instant in amazement, then burst into a peal of laughter.

" How ridiculous! But yes—they were intended for mine."

" How did they get into my luggage? "

" The woman who manages this inn placed them there. She is one of us."

" But what on earth for? "

" So that the police might find them when they searched your bags."

" Why should they search my bags? "

" There is a certain suspicion attaching to this place. It is impossible altogether to avoid it—so it is necessary to be very careful. The landlady thought that the discovery of the slippers might, in a measure, prepare the police for the arrival of your wife."

" Then she knew you were coming? "

" Certainly—since last night."

" And when the man who was to meet you did not arrive, she decided that I would do? "

" I suppose so."

" But how did she know I had a passport? "

" Perhaps you told her."

Yes, Stewart reflected, he had told her, and yet he was not altogether satisfied. When had he told her? Surely it was not until he returned from his tour of the town; then there was not time——

" Here is your passport," said his companion, abruptly breaking in upon his thoughts. " Fold it up and place it in your pocket. And do not find it too readily when the police ask for it. You must seem not to know exactly where it is. Also pack your belongings. Yes, you would better include the slippers. Meanwhile I shall try to make myself a little presentable," and she opened the tiny bag from which she had produced the pen.

" It seems to me," said Stewart, as he proceeded to obey, " that one pair of slippers and one pair of stockings is rather scanty baggage for a lady who has been at Spa for a month."

" My baggage went direct from Spa to Brussels," she answered from before the mirror, " in order to avoid the customs examination at the frontier. Have you any other questions ? "

" Only the big one as to who you really are, and where I'm going to see you again after you have delivered your report—and all that."

His back was toward her as he bent over his bags,

and he did not see the quick glance she cast at
him.

"It is impossible to discuss that now," she said,
hastily. "And I would warn you that the servant,
Hans, is a spy. Be very careful before him—be
careful always, until we are safe across the frontier.
There will be spies everywhere—a false word, a
false movement, and all may be lost. Are you
ready?"

Stewart, rising from buckling the last strap, found
himself confronting the most adorable girl he had
ever seen. Every trace of the journey had disappeared. Her cheeks were glowing, her eyes were
shining, and when she smiled, Stewart noticed a
dimple set diagonally at the corner of her mouth—
a dimple evidently placed just there to invite and
challenge kisses.

The admiration which flamed into his eyes was
perhaps a trifle too ardent, for, looking at him
steadily, she took a quick step toward him.

"We are going to be good friends, are we not?"
she asked. "Good comrades?"

And Stewart, looking down at her, understood.
She was pleading for respect; she was telling him
that she trusted him; she was reminding him of the
defenselessness of her girlhood, driven by hard

necessity into this strange adventure. And, understanding, he reached out and caught her hand.

"Yes," he agreed. "Good comrades. Just that!"

She gave his fingers a swift pressure.

"Thank you," she said. "Now we must go down. Dinner will be waiting. Fortunately the train is very late."

Stewart, glancing at his watch, saw that it was almost six o'clock.

"You are sure it is late?" he asked.

"Yes; at least an hour. We will send someone to inquire. Remember what I have told you about the waiter—about everyone. Not for an instant must we drop the mask, even though we may think ourselves unobserved. You will remember?"

"I will try to," Stewart promised. "But don't be disappointed if you find me a poor actor. I am not in your class at all. However, if you'll give me the cue, I think I can follow it."

"I know you can. Come," and she opened the door, restoring him the handkerchief which she had hung over the knob.

As they went down the stair together, Stewart saw the landlady waiting anxiously at the foot. One glance at them, and her face became radiant.

"Ah, you are late!" she cried, shaking a reproving finger. "But I expected it. I would not permit Hans to call you. When husband and wife meet after a long separation, they do not wish to be disturbed—not even for dinner. This way! I have placed the table in the court—it is much pleasanter there when the days are so warm," and she bustled before them to a vine-shaded corner of the court, where a snowy table awaited them.

A moment later Hans entered with the soup. Stewart, happening to meet his glance, read the suspicion there.

"Well," he said, breaking off a piece of the crisp bread, "this is almost like home, isn't it? I can't tell you, Mary, how glad I am to have you back again," and he reached out and gave her hand a little squeeze. "Looking so well, too. Spa was evidently just the place for you."

"Yes—it was very pleasant and the doctor was very kind. But I am glad to get back to you, Tommy," she added, gazing at him fondly. "I could weep with joy just to look at that honest face of yours!"

Stewart felt his heart skip a beat.

"You will make me conceited, if you don't take care, old lady!" he protested. "And surely I've got enough cause for conceit already, with the most beautiful woman in the world sitting across from me, telling me she loves me. Don't blame me if I lose my head a little!"

The ardor in his tone brought the color into her cheeks.

"You must not look at me like that!" she reproved. "People will think we are on our moon of —our honeymoon," she corrected, hastily.

"Instead of having been married four years! I wonder how John and Sallie are getting along? Aren't you just crazy to see the kids!"

She choked over her soup, but managed to nod mutely. Then, as Hans removed the plates and disappeared in the direction of the kitchen, he added in a lower tone, "You must allow me the children. I find I can't be happy without them!"

"Very well," she agreed, the dimple sparkling. "You have been so kind that it is impossible for me to refuse you anything!"

"There is one thing I can't understand. Your English astonishes me. Where did you learn to speak it so perfectly?"

"Ah, that is a long story! Perhaps I shall one day tell it to you—if we ever meet again."

"We must! I demand that as my reward!"

She held up a warning finger as steps sounded along the passage; but it was only the landlady bringing the wine. That good woman was exuberant —a trifle too exuberant, as Stewart's companion told her with a quick glance.

The dinner proceeded from course to course. Stewart had never enjoyed a meal more thoroughly. What meal, he asked himself, could possibly be commonplace, shared by such a woman?

The landlady presently dispatched Hans to the station to inquire about the train, while she herself did the serving, and the two women ventured to exchange a few words concerning their instructions. Stewart, listening, caught a glimpse of an intricate system of espionage extending to the very heart of Germany. But he asked no questions; indeed, some instinct held him back from wishing to know more. "Spy" is not a pretty word, nor is a spy's work pretty work; he refused to think of it in connection with the lovely girl opposite him.

"We shall have the police with us soon," said the landlady, in a low tone. "Hans will run at once to tell them of Madame's arrival."

"Why do you keep him?" Stewart asked.

"It is by keeping him that I avert suspicion. If there was anything wrong here, the police tell themselves, this spy of theirs would discover it. Knowing him to be a spy, I am on my guard. Besides, he is very stupid. But there—I will leave you. He may be back at any moment."

He came back just in time to serve the coffee, with the information that their train would not arrive until seven-thirty; then he stood watching them and listening to their talk of home and friends and plans for the future.

Stewart began to be proud of his facility of invention, and of his abilities as an actor. But he had to admit that he was the merest bungler compared with his companion. Her mental quickness dazzled him, her high spirits were far more exhilarating than the wine. He ended by forgetting that he was playing a part. This woman was really his wife, they were going on together——

Suddenly Hans stirred in his corner. Heavy steps were coming toward the court along the sanded floor of the corridor. In a moment three men in spiked helmets stepped out into the fading light of the evening.

" The police to speak to you, sir," said Hans, and Stewart, turning, found himself looking into three faces, in which hostility and suspicion were only too apparent.

CHAPTER VI

THE SNARE

As the three men advanced to the table, Stewart saw that each of them carried a heavy pistol in a holster at his belt.

" You speak German? " one of them asked, gruffly.

" A little. But I would prefer to speak English," answered Stewart.

" We will speak German. What is your nationality? "

" I am an American."

" Were you born in America? "

" Yes."

" Have you a passport? "

" Yes."

" Let me see it."

Stewart was about to reach into his pocket and produce it, when he remembered his companion's suggestion. So he felt in one pocket after another without result, while the Germans shifted impatiently from foot to foot.

"It must be in my other coat," he said, half to himself, enjoying the situation immensely. "But no; I do not remember changing it. Ah, here it is!" and he drew it forth and handed it to the officer.

The latter took it, unfolded it, and stepped out into the court where the light was better. He read it through carefully, compared the description point by point with Stewart's appearance, and then came back to the table.

"Who is this person?" he asked, and nodded toward the girl.

"She is my wife," answered Stewart, with a readiness which astonished himself.

"She did not arrive here with you."

"No," and he told the story of how he had left her at Spa to recuperate from a slight nervous attack, while he himself went on to Vienna. He omitted no detail—even added a few, indeed, in the fervor of creation—and with his limited German, which his hearers regarded with evident contempt, the story took some time to tell.

The police listened attentively to every word, without the slightest sign of impatience, but long before it was ended, the lady in question was twisting nervously in her seat.

"What is the matter, Tommy?" she demanded,

petulantly. "Are you relating to them the story of your life?"

"No," he explained, blandly, venturing at last to look at her, "I was just telling them how it was that you and I had arranged to meet at this hotel."

"Well—now tell them to go away. They are ugly and they annoy me."

"What does she say?" asked the officer.

Stewart was certain that at least one of them knew English, so he judged it best to translate literally.

"She wants to know what is the matter," he answered. "She asks me to tell you to go away—that you annoy her."

The officer smiled grimly.

"She does not understand German?"

"Not a word," lied Stewart, glibly.

"What is her name?"

"Mary."

"Her maiden name?"

"Mary Agnes Fleming," answered Stewart, repeating the first name that occurred to him, and thanking his stars the next instant that the officer could scarcely be acquainted with the lesser lights of English fiction.

"Is that correct?" asked the officer, suddenly turning upon her.

Stewart's heart gave a leap of fear; but after a stare at the officer, she turned to her companion.

"Was he speaking to me, Tommy?" she asked; and it was only by a heroic effort that Stewart choked back the sudden snort of laughter that rose in his throat.

"Yes," he managed to answer; "he wants to know your maiden name."

"Why should he wish to know that?"

"I give it up; but you'd better tell him."

"My maiden name was Mary Agnes Fleming," she said, looking at the officer with evident disapprobation. "Though what concern it is of yours I cannot see."

"What does she say?" demanded the officer, and again Stewart translated literally.

The officer stood staring intently at both of them, till the lady, with a flash of indignation, turned her back.

"Really, Tommy," she said, over her shoulder, "if you do not at once get rid of this brute, I shall never speak to you again!"

"He is a policeman, dear," Stewart explained, "and imagines that he is doing his duty. I suppose they *do* have to be careful in war-time. We must be patient."

" I will look at her passport," said the German, suddenly, and held out his hand.

" My passport is for both of us," Stewart explained. " Those words ' accompanied by his wife,' make it inclusive."

The officer went out into the light again and examined the words with minute attention.

" I find no description of her," he said, coming back.

" There is none," assented Stewart, impatiently; "but there is a description of me, as you see. The passport adds that I am accompanied by my wife. I tell you that this lady is my wife. That is sufficient."

The officer glanced at his companions uncertainly. Then he slowly folded up the passport and handed it back.

" When do you depart from Aachen? " he asked.

" By the first train for Brussels. I am told that it will arrive in about half an hour."

" Very well," said the other. " I regret if I have seemed insistent, but the fact that the lady did not arrive with you appeared to us singular. I will report your explanation to my chief," and he turned on his heel and stalked away, followed by his men.

Stewart drew a deep breath.

"Well," he began, when he was stopped by a sharp tap from his companion's foot.

"Such impudence!" she cried. "I was astonished at your patience, Tommy! You, an American, letting a Prussian policeman intimidate you like that! I am ashamed of you!"

Glancing around, Stewart saw the hang-dog Hans hovering in the doorway.

"He was a big policeman, my dear," he explained, laughing. "I shouldn't have had much of a chance with him, to say nothing of his two men. If we want to get to Brussels, the safest plan is to answer calmly all the questions the German police can think of. But it is time for us to be going. There will be no reserved seats on this train!"

"You are right," agreed his companion; "I am quite ready."

So he asked for the bill, paid it, sent Hans up for the luggage, and presently they were walking toward the station, with Hans staggering along behind.

Stewart, looking down at his companion, felt more and more elated over the adventure. He had never passed a pleasanter evening—it had just the

touch of excitement needed to give it relish. Unfortunately, its end was near; an hour or two in a
crowded railway carriage, and—that was all!

She glanced up at him and caught his eyes.

" What is it, my friend?" she asked. " You appear sad."

" I was just thinking," answered Stewart, " that
I do not even know your name!"

" Speak lower!" she said, quickly. "Or, better
still, do not say such things at all. Do not drop the
mask for an instant until we are out of Germany."

" Very well," Stewart promised. " But once we
are across the border, I warn you that I intend to
throw the mask away, and that I shall have certain
very serious things to say to you."

" And I promise to listen patiently," she answered,
smiling.

At the entrance to the station, they were stopped
by a guard, who demanded their tickets. Stewart
was about to produce his, when his companion
touched him on the arm.

" Hasten and get them, Tommy," she said. " I
will wait here."

And Stewart, as he hurried away, trembled to
think how nearly he had blundered. For how could
he have explained to the authorities the fact that he

was traveling with a book of Cook's circular tickets, while his wife was buying her tickets from station to station?

There was a long line of people in front of the ticket-office, and their progress was slow, for two police officers stood at the head of the line and interrogated every applicant for a ticket before they would permit it to be given him. Stewart, as he moved slowly forward, saw two men jerked violently out of the line and placed under arrest; he wondered uncomfortably if the officers had any instructions with regard to him, but, when his turn came, he faced them as unconcernedly as he was able. He explained that he and his wife were going to Brussels, showed his passport, and finally hastened away triumphant with the two precious bits of pasteboard. It seemed to him that the last difficulty had been encountered and overcome, and it was only by an effort that he kept himself from waving the tickets in the air as he rejoined his companion. In another moment, they were past the barrier. Hans was permitted to enter with them, and mounted guard over the luggage.

The platform was thronged with a motley and excited crowd, among whom were many officers in long gray coats and trailing swords, evidently on their way to join their commands. They were stalking up and down, with a lofty disregard for base civilians, talking loudly, gesticulating fiercely, and stopping ever and anon to shake hands solemnly. Stewart was watching them with an amusement somewhat too apparent, for his companion suddenly passed her arm through his.

" I should like to walk a little," she said. " I have been sitting too long." Then, in a lower tone, as they started along the platform, " It would be more wise not to look at those idiots. They would seek a quarrel with you in an instant if they suspected it was at them you were smiling."

" You are right," Stewart agreed; " besides, there is someone else whom I think much better worth looking at! The officers seem to share my opinion," he added, for more than one head was turned as they walked slowly down the platform. " I shall be jealous in a moment ! "

" Do not talk nonsense! Nothing is so absurd as for a man to make love to his wife in public ! "

Stewart would have liked to retort that he had, as yet, had mighty few opportunities in private, but he judged it best to save that remark for the other side of the frontier.

"Just the same," she rattled on, "it was good of you to write so regularly while you were at Vienna. I am sure your letters helped with my cure. But you have not told me—have you secured our passage?"

"I will know when we get to Brussels. Cook is trying to get us an outside room on the *Adriatic*."

"Do we go back to England?"

"Not unless we wish to. We can sail from Cherbourg."

They had reached the end of the platform, and, as they turned, Stewart found himself face to face with a bearded German who had been close behind them, and who shot a sharp glance at him and his companion before stepping aside with a muttered apology. Not until they had passed him did Stewart remember that he had seen the man before. It was the surly passenger in the crowded compartment on the journey from Cologne.

His companion had not seemed to notice the fellow, and went on talking of the voyage home and how glad she would be to get there. Not until they turned again at the farther end, and found the platform for a moment clear around them, did she relax her guard.

"That man is a spy," she whispered, quickly.

"We are evidently still suspected. What sort of railroad ticket have you?"

"A book of Cook's coupons."

"I feared as much. You must rid yourself of it— it is quite possible that you will be searched at the frontier. No, no," she added, as Stewart put his hand to his pocket. "Not here! You would be seen—everything would be lost. I will devise a way."

Stewart reflected with satisfaction that only a few coupons were left in the book. But why should he be searched? He had thought the danger over; but he began uneasily to suspect that it was just beginning. Well, it was too late to draw back, even had he wished to do so; and most emphatically he did not. He was willing to risk a good deal for another hour of this companionship—and then there was that explanation at the end—his reward——

There was a sharp whistle down the line, and the train from Cologne rolled slowly in.

"First class," said Stewart to Hans, as the latter picked up the luggage; and then he realized that they would be fortunate if they got into the train at all. The first five carriages were crowded with soldiers; then there were two carriages half-filled with officers, upon whom no one ventured to intrude.

The three rear carriages were already crowded with
a motley throng of excited civilians, and Stewart
had resigned himself to standing up, when Hans
shouted, " This way, sir; this way!" and started to
run as fast as the heavy suit-cases would permit.

Stewart, staring after him, saw that an additional
carriage was being pushed up to be attached to the
train.

" That fellow has more brains than I gave him
credit for," he said.   " Come along!"

Before the car had stopped, Hans, with a disregard of the regulations which proved how excited he
was, had wrenched open the door of the first compartment and clambered aboard.   By the time they
reached it, he had the luggage in the rack and sprang
down to the platform with a smile of triumph.

" Good work!" said Stewart.   " I didn't think
you had it in you!" and he dropped a generous tip
into the waiting hand.   " Come, my dear," and he
helped his companion aboard.   Hans slammed the
door shut after them, touched his cap, and hurried
away.   " Well, that was luck!" Stewart added, and
dropped to the seat beside his companion.   " But
look out for the deluge in another minute!"

She was looking out of the window at the excited
mob sweeping along the platform.

"The crowd is not coming this way," she said, after a moment. "A line of police is holding it back. I think this carriage is intended for the officers."

Stewart groaned.

"Then we shall have to get out! Take my advice and don't wait to be asked twice!"

"Perhaps they will not need this corner. In any case, we will stay until they put us out. If you are wise, you will forget all the German you know and flourish your passport frequently. Germans are always impressed by a red seal!"

But, strangely enough, they were not disturbed. A number of officers approached the carriage, and, after a glance at its inmates, passed on to the other compartments. Stewart, putting his head out of the window, saw that the line of police were still keeping back the crowd.

"Really," he said, "this seems too good to be true. It looks as if we were going to have this compartment to ourselves."

He turned smilingly to glance at her, and the smile remained frozen on his lips. For her face was deathly pale, her eyes were staring, and she was pressing her hands tight against her heart.

"You're not ill?" he asked, genuinely startled.

"Only very tired," she answered, controlling her voice with evident difficulty. "I think I shall try to rest a little," and she settled herself more comfortably in her corner. "The journey from Spa quite exhausted me." Then with her lips she formed the words "Be careful!"

"All right," said Stewart. "Go to sleep if you can."

She gave him a warning glance from under half-closed lids, then laid her head back against the cushions and closed her eyes.

Stewart, after a last look along the platform, raised the window half-way to protect his companion from the draft, then dropped into the corner opposite her and got out a cigar and lighted it with studied carelessness—though he was disgusted to see that his hand was trembling. He was tingling all over with the sudden sense of danger—tingling as a soldier tingles as he awaits the command to charge.

But what danger could there be? And then he thrilled at a sudden thought. Was this compartment intended as a trap? Had they been guided to it and left alone here in the hope that, thrown off their guard, they would in some way incriminate themselves? Was there an ear glued to some hole in the partition—the ear of a spy crouching in the next compartment?

Stewart pulled his hat forward over his eyes as though to shield them from the light. Then he went carefully back over the sequence of events which had led them to this compartment. It was Hans who had brought them to it—and Hans was a spy. It was he who had selected it, who had stood at the door so that they would go no farther. It was he who had slammed the door.

Was the door locked? Stewart's hand itched to try the handle; but he did not dare. Someone was perhaps watching as well as listening. But that they should be permitted to enter a carriage reserved for officers—that, on a train so crowded, they should be undisturbed in the possession of a whole compartment—yes, it was proof enough!

The station-master's whistle echoed shrilly along the platform, and the train glided slowly away.

Darkness had come, and as the train threaded the silent environs of the town, Stewart wondered why the streets seemed so gloomy. Looking again, he understood. Only a few of the street lights were burning. Already the economies of war had begun.

The train entered a long tunnel, at whose entrance a file of soldiers with fixed bayonets stood on guard.

At regular intervals, the light from the windows flashed upon an armed patrol. Farther on, a deep valley was spanned by a great viaduct, and here again there was a heavy guard. The valley widened, and suddenly as they swept around a curve, Stewart saw a broad plain covered with flaring lights. They were the lights of field-kitchens; and, looking at them, Stewart realized that a mighty army lay encamped here, ready to be hurled against the French frontier.

And then he remembered that this was not the French frontier, but the frontier of Belgium. Could the landlady of the Kölner Hof have been mistaken? To make sure, he got out his Baedeker and looked at the map. No; the French frontier lay away to the south. There was no way to reach it from this point save across Belgium. It was at Belgium, then, that the first blow was aimed—Belgium whose neutrality and independence had been guaranteed by all the Powers of Europe!

He put the book away and sat gazing thoughtfully out into the night. As far as the eye could reach gleamed the fires of the mighty bivouac. The army itself was invisible in the darkness, for the men had not thought it worth while to put up their shelter tents on so fine a night; but along the track, from time to time, passed a shadowy patrol ; once, as the train rolled above a road, Stewart saw that it was packed with transport wagons.

Then, suddenly, the train groaned to a stop.

"The frontier!" said Stewart to himself, and glanced at his companion, but she, to all appearance, was sleeping peacefully. "We shall be delayed here," he thought, "for the troops to detrain," and he lowered the window and put out his head to watch them do it.

The train had stopped beside a platform, and Stewart was astonished at its length. It stretched away and away into the distance, seemingly without end. And it was empty, save for a few guards.

The doors behind him were thrown open and the officers sprang out and hurried forward. From the windows in front of him, Stewart could see curious heads projecting; but the forward coaches gave no sign of life. Not a door was opened; not a soldier appeared.

"Where are we? What has happened?" asked his companion's voice, and he turned to find her rubbing her eyes sleepily.

"We are at the frontier, I suppose," he answered. "No doubt we shall go on as soon as the troops detrain."

" I hope they will not be long."

" They haven't started yet, but of course—by George!" he added, in another tone, " they aren't getting out! The guards are driving the people out of the cars ahead of us!"

The tumult of voices raised in angry protest drew nearer. Stewart could see that the carriages were being cleared, and in no gentle manner. There was no pause for explanation or argument—just a terse order which, if not instantly obeyed, was followed by action. Stewart could not help smiling, for, in that Babel of tongues, he distinguished a lot of un-expurgated American!

" There's no use getting into a fight with them," he said, philosophically, as he turned back into the compartment and lifted down his suit-cases. " We might as well get out before we're put out," and he tried to open the door.

It was locked.

The certainty that they were trapped turned him a little giddy.

" Who the devil could have locked this door? " he demanded, shaking the handle savagely.

" Seat yourself, Tommy," his companion advised. " Do not excite yourself—and have your passport ready. Perhaps they will not put us off."

And then a face, crowned by the ubiquitous spiked helmet, appeared at the window.

" You will have to get out," said the man in German, and tried to open the door.

Stewart shook his head to show that he didn't understand, and produced his passport.

The man waved it impatiently away, and wrenched viciously at the door, purple with rage at finding it locked. Then he shouted savagely at someone farther up the platform.

" I have always been told that the Germans were a phlegmatic people," observed Stewart; " but as a matter of fact, they blow up quicker and harder than anybody I ever saw. Look at that fellow, now——"

But at that moment a guard came running up, produced a key, and opened the door.

" Come, get out! " said the man, with a gesture there was no mistaking, and Stewart, picking up his bags, stepped out upon the platform and helped his companion to alight.

" How long will we be detained here? " he asked in English; but the man, with a contemptuous shrug, motioned him to stand back.

Looking along the platform, Stewart saw approaching the head of an infantry column. In a moment, the soldiers were clambering into the coaches, with the same mathematical precision he had seen before. But there was something unfamiliar in their appearance; and, looking more closely, Stewart saw that their spiked helmets were covered with gray cloth, and that not a button or bit of gilt glittered anywhere on the gray-green field uniforms. Wonderful forethought, he told himself. By night these troops would be quite invisible; by day they would be merged indistinguishably with the brown soil of the fields, the gray trunks of trees, the green of hedges.

The train rolled slowly out of the station, and Stewart saw that on the track beyond there was another, also loaded with troops. In a moment, it started westward after the first; and beyond it a third train lay revealed.

Stewart, glancing at his companion, was startled by the whiteness of her face, the steely glitter of her eyes.

" It looks like a regular invasion," he said. " But let us find out what's going to happen to us. We can't stand here all night. Good heavens—what is that ? "

From the air above them came the sudden savage whirr of a powerful engine, and, looking up, they saw a giant shape sweep across the sky. It was gone in an instant.

"A Zeppelin!" said Stewart, and felt within himself a thrill of wonder and exultation. Oh, this would be a great war! It would be like no other ever seen upon this earth. It would be fought in the air, as well as on the land; in the depths of the ocean, as well as on its surface. At last all theories were to be put to the supreme test!

· "You will come with me," said the man in the helmet, and Stewart, with a nod, picked up his grips again before he remembered that he was supposed to be ignorant of German.

"Did you say there was another train?" he asked. "Shall we be able to get away?"

The man shook his head and led the way along the platform, without glancing to the right or left. As they passed the bare little station, they saw that it was jammed to the doors with men and women and children, mixed in an indiscriminate mass, and evidently most uncomfortable. But their guide led them past it without stopping, and Stewart breathed a sigh of relief. Anything would be better than to be thrust into that crowd!

Again he had cause to wonder at the length of that interminable platform; but at last, near its farther end, their guide stopped before a small, square structure, whose use Stewart could not even guess, and flung open the door.

"You will enter here," he said.

"But look here," Stewart protested, "we are American citizens. You have no right——"

The man signed to them to hurry. There was something in the gesture which stopped the words on Stewart's lips.

"Oh, damn the fool!" he growled, swallowing hard. "Come along, my dear; there's no use to argue," and, bending his head at the low door, he stepped inside.

In an instant, the door was slammed shut, and the snap of a lock told them that they were prisoners.

CHAPTER VII

IN THE TRAP

As Stewart set down his bags, still swearing softly to himself, he heard behind him the sound of a stifled sob.

"There! there!" he said. "We'll soon be all right!" and as he turned swiftly and reached out his arms to grope for her, it seemed to him that she walked right into them.

"Oh, oh!" she moaned, and pressed close against him. "What will they do to us? Why have they placed us here?" And then he felt her lips against his ear. "Be careful!" she whispered in the merest breath. "There is an open window!"

Stewart's heart was thrilling. What a woman! What an actress! Well, he would prove that he, too, could play a part.

"They will do nothing to us, dear," he answered, patting her shoulder. "They will not dare to harm us! Remember, we are Americans!"

"But—but why should they place us here?"

"I don't know—I suppose they have to be careful. I'll appeal to our ambassador in the morning. He'll soon bring them to their senses. So don't worry!"

"But it is so dark!" she complained. "And I am so tired. Can we not seat ourselves somewhere?"

"We can sit on our bags," said Stewart. "Wait!" In a moment he had found them and placed them one upon the other. "There you are. Now let us see what sort of a place we've come to."

He got out his match-box and struck a light. The first flare almost blinded him; then, holding the match above his head, he saw they were in a brick cubicle, about twenty feet square. There was a single small window, without glass but heavily barred. The place was empty, save for a pile of barrels against one end.

"It's a store-house of some kind," he said, and then he sniffed sharply. "Gasoline! I'd better not strike any more matches."

He sat down beside her and for some moments they were silent. Almost unconsciously, his arm found its way about her waist. She did not draw away.

"Do you suppose they will keep us here all night?" she asked, at last.

"Heaven knows! They seem capable of any folly!"

And then again he felt her lips against his ear.

"We must destroy your ticket," she breathed. "Can you find it in the dark?"

"I think so." He fumbled in an inside pocket and drew it out. "Here it is."

Her groping hand found his and took the ticket.

"Now talk to me," she said.

Stewart talked at random, wondering how she intended to destroy the ticket. Once he fancied he heard the sound of soft tearing; and once, when she spoke in answer to a question, her voice seemed strange and muffled.

"It is done," she whispered at last. "Place these in your pocket and continue talking."

Her groping hand touched his and he found himself grasping two minute objects whose nature he could not guess, until, feeling them carefully, he found them to be the small wire staples which had held the coupons of the ticket together. He slipped them into his waistcoat pocket; and then, as he began to tell her about the women from Philadelphia and the journey from Cologne, he was conscious that she was no longer beside him. But at the end of a moment she was back again.

"That girl was perfectly right," she said. "Women are very silly to try to travel about Europe without a man as escort. Consider how I should feel at this moment if I did not have you!"

But in spite of themselves, the conversation lagged; and they finally sat silent.

How strange a thing was chance, Stewart pondered. Here was he who, until to-day, had seen his life stretching before him ordered and prosaic, cast suddenly into the midst of strange adventure. Here was this girl, whom he had known for only a few hours and yet seemed to have known for years —whom he certainly knew better than he had ever known any other woman There was Bloem—he had been cast into adventure, too. Was he outside somewhere, among all those thousands, gazing up at the stars and wondering at Fate? And the thousands themselves—the millions mustering at this moment into the armies of Europe—to what tragic adventure were they being hurried!

A quick step came along the platform and stopped at the door; there was the snap of a lock, and the door swung open.

"You will come out," said a voice in English.

Against the lights of the station, Stewart saw outlined the figure of a man in uniform. He rose wearily.

"Come, dear," he said, and helped her to her feet; "it seems we are to go somewhere else." Then he looked down at the heavy bags. "I can't carry those things all over creation," he said; "what's more, I won't."

"I will attend to that," said the stranger, and put a whistle to his lips and blew a shrill blast. Two men came running up. "You will take those bags," he ordered. "Follow me," he added to Stewart.

They followed him along the platform, crossed the track to another, and came at last to a great empty shed with a low table running along one side. The men placed the bags upon this table and withdrew.

"I shall have to search them," said the officer. "Are they locked?"

He stood in the glare of a lamp hanging from the rafters, and for the first time, Stewart saw his face. The man smiled at his start of surprise.

"I see you recognize me," he said. "Yes—I was in your compartment coming from Cologne. We will speak of that later. Are your bags locked?"

"No," said Stewart.

He watched with affected listlessness as the officer undid the straps and raised the lids. But his mind was very busy. Had he said anything during that ride from Cologne which he would now have reason to regret? Had he intimated that he was unmarried? He struggled to recall the conversation, sentence by sentence, but could remember nothing that was actually incriminating. And yet, in mentioning his intended stop at Aix-la-Chapelle, he had not added that he was to meet his wife there, and he had made a tentative arrangement to see Miss Field again in Brussels. The talk, in other words, had been carried on from the angle of a bachelor with no one to think of but himself, and not from that of a married man with a wife to consider.

It was certainly unfortunate that the man who had happened to overhear that conversation should be the one detailed here to examine his luggage. How well did he know English? Was he acute enough to catch the implications of the conversation, or would a disregard of one's wife seem natural to his Teutonic mind? Stewart glanced at him covertly; and then his attention was suddenly caught and held by the extreme care with which the man examined the contents of the bags.

He shook out each garment, put his hand in every

pocket, examined the linings with his finger-tips, ripped open one where he detected some unusual thickness only to discover a strip of reënforcement, opened and read carefully every letter and paper, turned the Baedeker page by page to be sure that nothing lay between them. He paused over the satin shoes and stockings, but put them down finally without comment. At last the bags were empty, and, taking up his knife, he proceeded to rip open the linen linings and look under them. Then, with equal care, he returned each article to its place, examining it a second time with the same intent scrutiny.

All this took time, and long before it was over, Stewart and his companion had dropped upon a bench which ran along the wall opposite the table. Stewart was so weary that he began to feel that nothing mattered very much, and he could see that the girl also was deadly tired. But at last the search was finished and the bags closed and strapped.

" I should like to see the small bag which Madame carries on her arm," said the officer, and, without a word, the girl held it out to him.

He examined its contents with a minuteness almost microscopic. Nothing was too small, too unimportant, to escape the closest attention. Stewart, marveling at this exhibition of German thoroughness, watched him through half-closed eyes, his heart beating a little faster. Would he find some clew, some evidence of treachery?

There were some handkerchiefs in the bag, and some small toilet articles; a cake of soap in a case, a box of powder, a small purse containing some gold and silver, a post-card, two or three letters, and some trivial odds and ends such as every woman carries about with her. The searcher unfolded each of the handkerchiefs and held it against the light, he cut the cake of soap into minute fragments; he emptied the box of powder and ran an inquiring finger through its contents; he turned out the purse and looked at every coin it contained; then he sat down and read slowly and gravely the postcard and each of the letters and examined their postmarks, and finally he took one of the closely-written sheets, mounted on his chair, and held the sheet close against the chimney of the lamp until it was smoking with the heat, examining it with minute attention as though he rather expected to make some interesting discovery. As a finish to his researches, he ripped open the lining of the bag and turned it inside out.

"Where did you buy this bag, madame?" he asked.

"In Paris, a month ago."

"These handkerchiefs are also French."

"Certainly. French handkerchiefs are the best in the world."

He compressed his lips and looked at her.

"And that is a French hat," he went on.

"Good heavens!" cried the girl. "One would think I was passing the customs at New York. Certainly it is French. So is my gown—so are my stockings—so is my underwear. For what else does an American woman come abroad?"

He looked at her shoes. She saw his glance and understood it.

"No; my shoes are American. The French do not know how to make shoes."

"But the slippers are French."

"Which slippers?"

"The ones in your husband's bag."

She turned laughingly to Stewart.

"Have you been carrying a pair of my slippers all around Europe, Tommy?" she asked. "How did that happen?"

"I don't know. I packed in rather a hurry," answered Stewart, sheepishly.

"Where is the remainder of your baggage, madame?" asked the officer.

"At Brussels—at least, I hope so. I sent it there direct from Spa."

"Why did you do that?"

"In order to avoid the examination at the frontier."

"Why did not you yourself go direct to Brussels?"

"I wished to see my husband. I had not seen him for almost a month," and she cast Stewart a fond smile.

"Have you been recently married?"

"We have been married four years," the girl informed him, with dignity.

Stewart started to give some additional information about the family, but restrained himself.

The inspector looked at them both keenly for a moment, scratching his bearded chin reflectively. Then he took a rapid turn up and down the shed, his brow furrowed in thought.

"I shall have to ask you both to disrobe," he said, at last, and as Stewart started to his feet in hot protest, he added, quickly, "I have a woman who will disrobe Madame."

"But this is an outrage!" protested Stewart, his face crimson. "This lady is my wife—I won't stand by and see her insulted. I warn you that you are making a serious mistake."

" She shall not be insulted. Besides, it is necessary."

" I don't see it."

" That is for me to decide," said the other bluntly, and he put his whistle to his lips and blew two blasts.

A door at the farther end of the shed opened and a woman entered. She was a matronly creature with a kind face, and she smiled encouragingly at the shrinking girl.

" Frau Ritter," said the officer in German, " you will take this lady into the office and disrobe her. Bring her clothing to me here—all of it."

Again Stewart started to protest, but the officer silenced him with a gesture.

" It is useless to attempt resistance," he said, sharply. " I must do my duty—by force if necessary. It will be much wiser to obey quietly."

The girl rose to her feet, evidently reassured by the benevolent appearance of the woman.

" Do not worry, Tommy," she said. " It will be all right. It is of no use to argue with these people. There is nothing to do but submit."

" So it seems," Stewart muttered, and watched her until she disappeared through the door.

"Now, sir," said the officer, sharply, "your clothes."

Crimson with anger and humiliation, Stewart handed them over piece by piece, saw pockets turned out, linings loosened here and there, the heels of his shoes examined, his fountain-pen unscrewed and emptied of its ink. At last he stood naked under the flaring light, feeling helpless as a baby.

"Well, I hope you are satisfied," he said, vindictively.

With a curt nod, the officer handed him back his underwear.

"I will keep these for the moment," he said, indicating the little pile of things taken from the pockets. "You may dress. *Your* clothes, at least, are American!"

As he spoke, the woman entered from the farther door, with a bundle of clothing in her arms. Stewart turned hastily away, struggling into his trousers as rapidly as he could, and cursing the careless immodesty of these people. Sullenly he laced his shoes, and put on his collar, noting wrathfully that it was soiled. He kept his back to the man at the table—he felt that it would be indecent to watch him scrutinizing those intimate articles of apparel.

"You have examined her hair?" he heard the man ask.

"Yes, Excellency."

"Very well; you may take these back."

Not until he heard the door close behind her did Stewart turn around. The officer was lighting a cigarette. The careless unconcern of the act added new fuel to the American's wrath.

"Perhaps you will tell me the meaning of all this?" he demanded. "Why should my wife and I be compelled to submit to these indignities?"

"We are looking for a spy," replied the other imperturbably, and addressed himself to an examination of the things he had taken from Stewart's pockets—his penknife, his watch, the contents of his purse, the papers in his pocket-book. He even placed a meditative finger for an instant on the two tiny metal clips which had come from the Cook ticket. But to reconstruct their use was evidently too great a task even for a German police agent, for he passed on almost at once to something else. "Very good," he said at last, pushed the pile toward its owner, and opened the passport, which he had laid to one side.

"That passport will tell you that I am not a spy," said Stewart, putting his things angrily back into his pockets. "That, it seems to me, should be sufficient."

"As far as you are concerned, it is entirely sufficient," said the other. "One can see at a glance that you are an American. But the appearance of Madame is distinctly French."

"Americans are of every race," Stewart pointed out. "I have seen many who look far more German than you do."

"That is true; but it so happens that the spy we are looking for is a woman. I cannot tell you more, except that it is imperative she does not escape."

"And you suspect my wife?" Stewart demanded. "But that is absurd!"

He was proud of the fact that he had managed to maintain unaltered his expression of virtuous indignation, for a sudden chill had run down his spine at the other's careless words. Evidently the situation was far more dangerous than he had suspected! Then he was conscious that his hands were trembling slightly, and thrust them quickly into his pockets.

"The fact that she joined you at Aachen seemed most suspicious," the inspector pointed out. "I do not remember that you mentioned her during your conversation with the ladies in the train."

" Certainly not. Why should I have mentioned her? "

" There was perhaps no reason for doing so," the inspector admitted. " Nevertheless, it seemed to us unusual that she should have come back from Spa to Aachen to meet you, when she might, so much more conveniently, have gone direct to Brussels and awaited you there."

" She has explained why we made that arrangement."

" Yes," and through half-closed eyes he watched the smoke from his cigarette circle upwards toward the lamp. " Conjugal affection—most admirable, I am sure! It is unfortunate that Madame's appearance should answer so closely to that of the woman for whom we are searching. It was also unfortunate that you should have met at the Kölner Hof. That hotel has not a good reputation—it is frequented by too many French whose business is not quite clear to us. How did it happen that you went there? "

" Why," retorted Stewart hotly, glad of the chance to return one of the many blows which had been rained upon him, " one of your own men recommended it."

" One of my own men? I do not understand," and the officer looked at him curiously.

" At least one of the police. He came to me at the Hotel Continental at Cologne to examine my passport. He asked me where I was going from Cologne, and I told him to Aix-la-Chapelle. He asked at which hotel I was going to stay, and I said I did not know. He said he would like to have that information for his report, and added that the Kölner Hof was near the station and very clean and comfortable. I certainly found it so."

The officer was listening with peculiar intentness.

" Why were you not at the station to meet your wife? " he asked.

" I did not know when she would arrive; I was told that the trains were all running irregularly," answered Stewart, prouder of his ability to lie well and quickly than he had ever been of anything else in his life.

" But how did she know at which hotel to find you? " inquired the officer, and negligently flipped the ash from his cigarette.

Stewart distinctly felt his heart turn over as he saw the abyss at his feet. How would she have known? How *could* she have known? What would he have done if he had really had a wife waiting at Spa? These questions flashed through his head like lightning.

"Why, I telegraphed her, of course," he said; "and to make assurance doubly sure, I sent her a postcard." And then his heart fell again, for he realized that the police had only to wire to Cologne to prove that no such message had been filed there.

But the officer tossed away his cigarette with a little gesture of satisfaction.

"It was well you took the latter precaution, Mr. Stewart," he said, and Stewart detected a subtle change in his tone—it was less cold, more friendly. "The wires were closed last night to any but official business, and your message could not possibly have got through. I am surprised that it was accepted."

"I gave it to the porter at the hotel," Stewart explained. "Perhaps it wasn't accepted, and he just kept the money."

"That may be. But your postcard got through, as you no doubt know. It evidently caught the night mail and was delivered to Madame this morning."

"Really," stammered Stewart, wondering desperately if this was another trap, "I didn't know—I didn't think to ask——"

"Luckily Madame brought it with her in her hand-bag," explained the other. "It offers a convincing confirmation of your story—the more convincing perhaps since you seem surprised that she preserved it. Ah, here she is now," and he arose as the door opened and the girl came in. "Will you not sit down, madame?" he went on, courteously. " I pray that both of you will accept my sincere apologies for the inconvenience I have caused you. Believe me, it was one of war's necessities."

The girl glanced at the speaker curiously, his tone was so warm, so full of friendship; then she glanced at Stewart——

And Stewart, catching that glance, was suddenly conscious that his mouth was open and his eyes staring and his whole attitude that of a man struck dumb by astonishment. Hastily he bent over to retie a shoestring. But really, he told himself, he could not be blamed for being disconcerted—anybody would be disconcerted to be told suddenly that his most desperate lie was true! But how could it be true? How could there be any such postcard as the German had described? Was it just another trap?

" We understand, of course, that you were merely doing your duty," the girl's voice was saying; " what seemed unfair was that we should be the victims. Do I understand that—that you no longer suspect us?"

"Absolutely not; and I apologize for my suspicions."

"Then we are at liberty to proceed?"

"You cannot in any event proceed to-night. I will pass you in the morning. And I hope you will not think that any discourtesy was intended to you as Americans. Germany is most anxious to retain the good-will of America. It will mean much to us in this struggle."

"Most Americans are rather sentimental over Alsace-Lorraine," said Stewart, who had recovered his composure, and he fished for a cigar and offered one to the officer, who accepted it with a bow of thanks.

"That is because they do not understand," said the other, quickly. "Alsace and Lorraine belong of right to Germany. Of that there can be no question."

"But haven't you been rather harsh with them?"

"We have not been harsh enough. Had we done our duty, we would have stamped out without mercy the treason which is still rampant in many parts of those provinces. Instead, we have hesitated, we have temporized—and now, too late, we realize our mistake. The spy for whom we are searching at this moment comes from Strassburg."

Stevart started at the words; but the girl threw back her head and burst into delighted laughter.

"So you took us for spies!" she cried. "What a tale to tell, Tommy, when we get home!"

"There is but one spy, madame," said the officer; "a woman young and beautiful like yourself—accomplished, distinguished, a great linguist, a fine musician, of good family, and moving in the highest society in Alsace. She was on terms of intimacy with many of our officers; they did not hesitate to talk freely to her. Some of them, fascinated by her wit and beauty and wishing to prove their own importance, told her things which they had no right to tell. More than that, at the last moment she succeeded in getting possession for a time of certain confidential documents. But she had gone too far— she was suspected—she fled—and she has not yet been captured. But she cannot escape—we cannot permit her to escape. We know that she is still somewhere in Germany, and we have made it impossible for her to pass the frontier. A person who knows her is to be stationed at every post, and no woman will be permitted to pass until he has seen her. The man to be stationed here will arrive from Strassburg in an hour. As a final precaution,

madame," he added, smiling, "and because my orders are most precise and stringent, I shall ask you
and your husband to remain here at Herbesthal until
morning. As I have said, you could not, in any
event, go on to-night, for the frontier is closed. In
the morning, I will ask my man from Strassburg to
look at you, and will then provide you with a safe-
conduct, and see that every possible facility is given
you to get safely across the frontier."

"Thank you," she said; "you are most kind.
That is why you are keeping all those people shut up
in the station?"

"Yes, madame. They cannot pass until my man
has seen them."

"But you are not searching them?"

"No; with most of them, the detention is a mere
matter of obeying orders—one can tell their nationality at a glance. But to look at you, madame,
I should never have supposed you to be an American
—I should have supposed you to be French."

"My grandmother was French," explained the
girl, composedly, "and I am said to resemble her
very closely. I must also warn you that my sym-
pathies are French."

The officer shrugged his shoulders with a smile.

"That is a great misfortune. Perhaps when you

see how our army fights, we may claim some of your sympathy—or, at least, your admiration."

" It will fight well, then? "

" It will fight so well—it will prove so irresistible—that our General Staff has been able to prepare in advance the schedule for the entire campaign. This is the first of August. On the fifth we shall capture Lille, on the ninth we shall cross the Marne, and on the eleventh we shall enter Paris. On the evening of the twelfth, the Emperor will dine the General Staff at the Ritz."

Stewart stared in astonishment, not knowing whether to laugh or to be impressed. But there was no shadow of a smile on the bearded face of the speaker.

" You are not in earnest! " Stewart protested.

" Thoroughly in earnest. We know where we shall be at every hour of every day. There are at present living in France many Germans who are reservists in our army. Not one of these has been required to return to Germany. On the contrary, each of them has been instructed to report at a point near his place of residence at a certain hour of a certain day, where he will find his regiment awaiting him. For example, all German reservists living at Lille, or in the neighborhood, will report at noon of Wednesday next in the Place de la République in front of the prefecture, where the German administration will have been installed during the morning."

Stewart opened his lips to say something, but no words came. He felt intimidated and overborne.

But it was not at Stewart the officer was looking so triumphantly, it was at the girl. Perhaps he also, yielding to a subtle fascination, was telling things he had no right to tell in order to prove his importance!

The girl returned his gaze with a look of astonishment and admiration.

" How wonderful! " she breathed.   " And it is really true? "

" True in every detail, madame."

" But this Lille of which you have spoken—is it a fortress? "

" A great fortress, madame."

" Will it not resist? "

" Not for long—perhaps not at all. If it does resist, it will fall like a house of cards. The whole world will be astonished, madame, when it learns the details of that action. We have a great surprise in store for our enemies! "

Stewart, glancing at his companion, noted with alarm the flash of excitement in her eyes. Would she push her questioning too far—would she be indiscreet; but the next instant he was reassured.

"It is most fascinating,—this puzzle!" she laughed. "I shall watch the papers for the fall of Lille. But I am very ignorant—I do not even know where Lille is."

"It is in the northwest corner of France, madame, just south of the Belgian frontier."

The girl looked at him perplexedly.

"But how can you reach it," she asked, slowly, "without crossing Belgium?"

"We cannot reach it without crossing Belgium."

From the expression of her face, she might have been a child shyly interrogating an indulgent senior.

"I know I am stupid," she faltered, "but it seems to me I have read somewhere—perhaps in Baedeker —that all the Powers had agreed that Belgium should always be a neutral country."

"So they did—Germany as well as the others. But such agreements are mere scraps of paper. The first blast of war blows them away. France has built along her eastern border a great chain of forts which are almost impregnable. Therefore it is necessary for us to strike her from the north through Belgium. Regretfully, but none the less firmly, we have warned Belgium to stand aside."

" Will she stand aside? "

The officer shrugged his shoulders.

" She must, or risk annihilation. She will not dare oppose us. If she does, we shall crush her into the dust. She will belong to us, and we will take her. Moreover, we shall not repeat the mistake we made in Alsace-Lorraine. There will be no treason in Belgium! "

Stewart felt a little shiver of disgust sweep over him. So this was the German attitude—treaties, solemn agreements, these were merely " scraps of paper " not worth a second thought; a small nation had no rights worth considering, since it lacked the power to defend them. Should it try to do so, it would " risk annihilation! "

He did not feel that he could trust himself to talk any longer, and rose suddenly to his feet.

" What are we going to do to-night? " he asked. " Not sit here in this shed, surely! "

" Certainly not," and the officer rose too. " I have secured a lodging for you with the woman who searched Madame. You will find it clean and comfortable, though by no means luxurious."

" That is very kind of you," said Stewart, with a memory of the rabble he had seen crowded into the waiting-room. And then he looked at his luggage.

"I hope it isn't far," he added. "I've carried those bags about a thousand miles to-day."

"It is but a step—but I will have a man carry your bags. Here is your passport, sir, and again permit me to assure you of my regret. You also, madame!" and he bowed ceremoniously above her fingers.

Three minutes later, Stewart and his companion were walking down the platform beside the pleasant-faced woman, who babbled away amiably in German, while a porter followed with the bags. As they passed the station, they could see that it was still jammed with a motley crowd, while a guard of soldiers thrown around it prevented anyone leaving or entering.

"How fortunate that we have escaped that!" said Stewart. "Even at the price of being searched!"

"This way, sir," said the woman, in German, and motioned off into the darkness to the right.

They made their way across a net-work of tracks, which seemed to Stewart strangely complicated and extensive for a small frontier station, and then emerged into a narrow, crooked street, bordered by mean little houses. In front of one of these the woman stopped and unlocked the door with an enormous key. The porter set the bags inside, received his tip, and withdrew, while their hostess struck a match and lighted a candle, disclosing a narrow hall running from the front door back through the house.

"You will sleep here, sir," she said, and opened a door to the left.

They stepped through, in obedience to her gesture, and found themselves in a fair-sized room, poorly furnished and a little musty from disuse, but evidently clean. Their hostess hastened to open the window and to light another candle. Then she brought in Stewart's bags.

"You will find water there," and she pointed to the pitcher on the wash-stand. "I cannot give you hot water to-night—there is no fire. Will these towels be sufficient? Yes? Is there anything else? No? Then good-night, sir, and you also, my lady."

"Good-night," they answered; and for a moment after the door closed, stood staring at it as though hypnotized.

Then the girl stepped to the window and pulled together the curtains of white cotton. As she turned back into the room, Stewart saw that her face was livid.

His eyes asked the question which he did not dare speak aloud.

She drew him back into the corner and put her lips close against his ear.

" There is a guard outside," she whispered. " We must be very careful. We are prisoners still."

As Stewart stood staring, she took off her hat and tossed it on a chair.

"How tired I am!" she said, yawning heavily, and turning back to the window, she began to take down her hair.

CHAPTER VIII

PRESTO! CHANGE!

THE vision of that dark hair rippling down as she drew out pin after pin held Stewart entranced. And the curve of her uplifted arms was also a thing to be remembered! But what was it she proposed to do? Surely——

" If you are going to wash, you would better do it, Tommy," she said, calmly. " I shall be wanting to in a minute."

Mechanically, Stewart slipped out of his coat, undid his tie; took off his collar, pulled up his sleeves, and fell to. He was obsessed by a feeling of un-reality which even the cold water did not dissipate. It couldn't be true—all this——

" I wish you would hurry, Tommy," said a voice behind him. " I am waiting for you to unhook my bodice."

Stewart started round as though stung by an adder. His companion's hair fell in beautiful dark waves about her shoulders, and he could see that her bodice was loosened.

"There are two hooks I cannot reach," she explained, in the most matter-of-fact tone. "I should think you would know that by this time!"

"Oh, so it's *that* bodice!" said Stewart, and dried his hands vigorously, resolved to play the game to the end, whatever it might be. "All right," and as she turned her back toward him, he began gingerly searching for the hooks.

"Come a little this way," she said; "you can see better," and, glancing up, Stewart suddenly understood.

They were standing so that their shadows fell upon the curtain. The comedy was being played for the benefit of the guard in the street outside.

The discovery that it *was* a comedy gave him back all his aplomb, and he found the hooks and disengaged them with a dexterity which no real husband could have improved upon.

"There," he said; "though why any woman should wear a gown so fashioned that she can neither dress nor undress herself passes my comprehension. Why not put the hooks in front?"

"And spoil the effect? Impossible! The hooks must be in the back," and still standing before the window, she slowly drew her bodice off.

Stewart had seen the arms of many women, but

never a pair so rounded and graceful and beautiful as those at this moment disclosed to him. Admirable too was the way in which the head was set upon the lovely neck, and the way the neck itself merged into the shoulders—the masterpiece of a great artist, so he told himself.

" I wonder if there is a shutter to that window? " she asked, suddenly, starting round toward it. " If there is, you would better close it. Somebody might pass—besides, I do not care to sleep on the ground-floor of a strange house in a strange town, with an open window overlooking the street! "

" I'll see," said Stewart, and pulling back the curtains, stuck out his head. " Yes—there's a shutter— a heavy wooden one." He pulled it shut and pushed its bolt into place. " There; now you're safe! "

She motioned him quickly to lower the window, and this he did as noiselessly as possible.

" Was there anyone outside? " she asked, in a low tone.

He shook his head. The narrow street upon which the window opened had seemed quite deserted —but the shadows were very deep.

" I wish you would open the bags," she said, in her natural voice. " I shall have to improvise a night-dress of some sort."

Although he knew quite well that the words had been uttered for foreign consumption, as it were, Stewart found that his fingers were trembling as he undid the straps and threw back the lids, for he was quite unable to guess what would be the end of this strange adventure or to what desperate straits they might be driven by the pressure of circumstance.

"There you are," he said, and sat down and watched her.

She knelt on the floor beside the bags and turned over their contents thoughtfully, laying to one side a soft outing shirt, a traveling cap, a lounging coat, a pipe and pouch of tobacco, a handful of cigars, a pair of trousers, a belt, three handkerchiefs, a pair of scissors. She paused for a long time over a pair of Stewart's shoes, but finally put them back with a shake of the head.

"No," said Stewart, "I agree with you. Shoes are not necessary to a sleeping costume. But then neither is a pipe."

She laughed.

"You will find that the pipe is very necessary," she said, and rising briskly, stepped to the wash-stand and gave face and hands and arms a scrubbing so vigorous that she emerged, as it seemed to Stewart, more radiant than ever. Then she glanced into the pitcher with an exclamation of dismay. "There! I have used all the water! I wonder if our landlady has gone to bed?"

Catching up the pitcher, she crossed rapidly to the door and opened it. There was no one there, and Stewart, following with the candle, saw that the hall was empty. They stood for a moment listening, but not a sound disturbed the stillness of the house.

The girl motioned him back into the room and closed the door softly. Then, replacing the pitcher gently, she caught up a pile of Stewart's socks and stuffed them tightly under the door. Finally she set a chair snugly against it—for there was no lock—and turned to Stewart with a little sigh of relief.

"There," she said in a low tone; "no one can see our light nor overhear us, if we are careful. Perhaps they really do not suspect us—but we must take no chances. What hour have you?"

Stewart glanced at his watch.

"It is almost midnight."

"There is no time to lose. We must make our plans. Sit here beside me," and she sat down in one corner against the wall. "We must not waste our candle," she added. "Bring it with you, and we will blow it out until we need it again."

Stewart sat down beside her, placed the candle on the floor and leaned forward and blew it out.

For a moment they sat so, quite still, then Stewart felt a hand touch his. He seized it and held it close.

"I am very unhappy, my friend," she said, softly, "to have involved you in all this."

"Why, I am having the time of my life!" Stewart protested.

"If I had foreseen what was to happen," she went on, "I should never have asked you to assist me. I would have found some other way."

"The deuce you would! Then I'm glad you didn't foresee it."

"It is good of you to say so; but you must not involve yourself further."

"What do you mean by that?"

"I am in great danger. It is absolutely necessary that I escape. I cannot remain till morning. I cannot face that inspection. I should be denounced."

"Yes," agreed Stewart; "that's clear enough."

"Well, I will escape alone. When the police come for us, they will find only you."

"And will probably back me against a wall and shoot me out of hand."

"Oh, no; they will be rough and angry, but they will not dare to harm you. They know that you are an American—they cannot possibly suspect you of being a spy. You can prove the truth of all your statements."

"Not quite all," Stewart corrected.

"Of your statements, at least, so far as they concern yourself."

"Yes—but I will have considerable difficulty explaining my connection with you."

"Oh, no," said the girl, in a low voice; "that can be easily explained."

"How?"

"You will say," she answered, her voice lower still, "that you met me at the Kölner Hof, that I made advances, that you found me attractive, and that I readily agreed to accompany you to Paris. You can say that it was I who suggested altering your passport—that you saw no harm in it—and that you knew absolutely nothing about me except that I was a—a loose woman."

Stewart's lips were trembling so that it was a moment before he could control his voice.

"And do you really think I would say that, little comrade?" he asked, hoarsely. "Do you really think anything on earth could compel me to say that!"

He heard the quick intake of her breath; then she raised his hand to her cheek and he felt the hot tears upon it.

"Don't you understand," he went on earnestly, "that we are in this together to the end—the very end? I know I'm not of much use, but I am not such a coward as you seem to think me, and——"

She stopped him with a quick pressure of the fingers.

"Don't!" she breathed. "You are cruel!"

"Not half so cruel as you were a moment ago," he retorted.

"Forgive me, my friend," she pleaded, and moved a little nearer. "I did not know—I am but a girl— I thought perhaps you would wish to be rid of me."

"I don't want ever to be rid of you," began Stewart, brokenly, drawing her closer. "I don't want ever——"

She yielded for an instant to his arm; for the fraction of an instant her head was upon his breast; then she drew herself away, and silenced him with a tap upon the lips.

"Not now!" she said, and her voice, too, was

hoarse. "All we must think of now is to escape. Afterwards, perhaps——"

"I shall hold you to that!" said Stewart, and released her.

But again for an instant she bent close.

"You are a good man!" she whispered.

"Oh, no!" Stewart protested, though he was shaken by the words. "No better than the average!"

And then he suddenly found himself unable to go on, and there was a moment's silence. When he spoke again, he had regained his self-control.

"Have you a plan?" he asked.

"Yes," she said, and drew a quick breath, as of one shaking away some weakness. "The first part is that you should sit quite still until I tell you to light the candle."

"But what——"

"A good soldier does not ask questions."

"All right, general," said Stewart, and settled back against the wall, completely, ineffably happy. Never before, he told himself, had he known what happiness was; never before had the mere joy of living surged through his veins as it was doing now. Little comrade! But what was she doing?

He could hear her moving softly about the room;

he could hear the rustle of what he took to be the bed-clothes; then the bed creaked as she sat down upon it. What was she doing? Why should she work in the dark, alone, without asking him to help? Was it because he could not help—was of so little use——

" You may light the candle now, my friend," she said, in a low voice.

Stewart had a match ready—had had it ready for long minutes!—and in a trice the wick was alight and the flame shot up clear and steady.

After one glance, he sprang in amazement to his feet, for there before him stood a youth—the handsomest he had ever seen—Peter Pan come to earth again!—his hand at the visor of his traveling-cap in mock salute.

" Well! " said Stewart, after a moment of amazed and delighted silence. " I believe you are a witch! Let me look at you! " and he caught up the candle and held it above his head.

The face upturned to his flamed crimson at the wonder and admiration in his eyes, but the dimple was sparkling at the corner of her mouth as she turned obediently before him and stepped slowly across the room. There is at the heart of every woman, however virginal and innocent, a subtle delight in knowing that men find her beautiful, and there could be no question of what Stewart thought at this moment.

At last she came to a stop facing him.

"Well?" she asked. "Will I do?"

"Will you do?" Stewart echoed, and Meredith's phrase recurred to him—"an imp in porcelain"— how perfectly it described her! "You are entirely, absolutely, impeccably—oh, I haven't adjectives enough! Only I wish I had a hundred candles instead of one!"

"But the clothes," she said, and looked doubtfully down at them. "Do I look like a boy?"

"Not in the least!" he answered, promptly.

Her face fell.

"But then——"

"Perhaps it is just because I know you're not one," he reassured her. "Let me see if I can improve matters. The trousers are too large, especially about the waist. They seem in danger of—hum!" and indeed she was clutching them desperately with one hand. "We will make another hole in that belt about three inches back," and he got out his knife and suited the action to the word. "There— that's better—you can let go of them now! And we'll turn up the legs about four inches—no, we'd better cut them off." He set the candle on the floor, picked up the scissors, and carefully trimmed each leg. " But those feet are ridiculous," he added, severely. " No real boy ever had feet like that!"

She stared down at them ruefully.

" They will seem larger when I get them full of mud," she pointed out. " I thought of putting on a pair of your shoes, but gave it up, for I am afraid I could not travel very far in them. Fortunately these are very strong!"

He sniffed skeptically, but had to agree with her that his shoes were impossible.

" There is one thing more," and she lifted her cap and let her tucked-up hair fall about her shoulders. " This must be cut off."

" Oh, no," protested Stewart, drawing back in horror. " That would be desecration—why, it's the most beautiful hair in the world!"

" Nonsense! In any case, it will grow again."

" Why not just tie it up under your cap?"

But she shook her head.

" No—it must come off. I might lose the cap— you see it is too large—and my hair would betray us. Cut it off, my friend—be quick."

She was right, of course, and Stewart, with a heavy heart, snipped away the long tresses. Then he trimmed the hair as well as he was able—which was very badly indeed. Finally he parted it rakishly on one side—and only by a supreme effort restrained himself from taking her in his arms and kissing her.

"Really," he said, "you're so ridiculously lovely that I'm in great danger of violating our treaty. I warn you it is extremely dangerous to look at me like that!"

She lowered her eyes instantly, but she could not restrain the dimple. Luckily, in the shadow, Stewart did not see it.

"We must make my clothing into a bundle," she said, sedately. "I may need it again. Besides, these people must not suspect that I have gone away disguised like this. That will give us a great advantage. Yes, gather up the hair and we will take it too—it would betray us. Put the cigars in your pocket. I will take the pipe and tobacco."

"Do you expect to smoke? I warn you that that pipe is a seasoned one!"

"I may risk a puff or two. I have been told there is no passport like a pipe of tobacco. No—do not shut the bags. Leave them open as though we had fled hurriedly. And," she added, crimsoning a little,

"I think it would be well to disarrange the bed."

Stewart flung back the covers and rolled upon it, while his companion cast a last look about the room. Then she picked up her little bag and took out the purse and the two letters.

"Which pocket of a man's clothes is safest?" she asked.

"The inside coat pocket. There are two inside pockets in the coat you have on. One of them has a flap which buttons down. Nothing could get out of it."

She took the coins from the purse, dropped them into the pocket, and replaced the purse in the bag. Then she started to place the letters in the pocket, but hesitated, looking at him searchingly, her lips compressed.

"My friend," she said, coming suddenly close to him and speaking in the merest breath, "I am going to trust you with a great secret. The information I carry is in these letters—apparently so innocent. If anything should happen to me——"

"Nothing is going to happen to you," broke in Stewart, roughly. "That is what I am for!"

"I know—and yet something may. If anything should, promise me that you will take these letters from my pocket, and by every means in your power, seek to place them in the hands of General Joffre."

"General Joffre?" repeated Stewart. "Who is he?"

"He is the French commander-in-chief."

"But what chance would I have of reaching him? I should merely be laughed at if I asked to see him!"

"Not if you asked in the right way," and again she hesitated. Then she pressed still closer. "Listen—I have no right to tell you what I am about to tell you, and yet I must. Do you remember at Aix, I looked at you like this?" and she caught her lower lip for an instant between the thumb and little finger of her left hand.

"Yes, I remember; and you burst into tears immediately afterward."

"That was because you did not understand. If, in answer, you had passed your left hand across your eyes, I should have said, in French, ' Have we not met before?' and if you had replied, ' In Berlin, on the twenty-second,' I should have known that you were one of ours. Those passwords will take you to General Joffre himself."

"Let us repeat them," Stewart suggested. In a moment he knew them thoroughly. "And *that's* all right!" he said.

"You consent, then?" she asked, eagerly.

"To assist you in every way possible—yes."

"To leave me, if I am not able to go on; to take the letters and press on alone," she insisted, her eyes shining. "Promise me, my friend!"

"I shall have to be governed by circumstances," said Stewart, cautiously. "If that seems the best thing to do—why, I'll do it, of course. But I warn you that this enterprise would soon go to pieces if it had no better wits than mine back of it. Why, in the few minutes they were searching you back there at the station, I walked straight into a trap—and with my eyes wide open, too—at the very moment when I was proudly thinking what a clever fellow I was!"

"What was the trap?" she asked, quickly.

"I was talking to that officer, and babbled out the story of how I came to go to the Kölner Hof, and he seemed surprised that a member of the police should have recommended it—which seems strange to me, too," he added, "now that I think of it. Then he asked me suddenly how you knew I was there."

"Yes, yes; and what did you say?"

"I didn't say anything for a minute—I felt as though I were falling out of a airship. But after

I had fallen about a mile, I managed to say that I
had sent you a telegram and also a postcard."

" How lucky! " breathed the girl. " How shrewd
of you! "

" Shrewd? Was it? But that shock was nothing
to the jolt I got the next minute when he told me
that you had brought the postcard along in your
bag! It was a good thing you came in just then,
or he would have seen by the way I sat there gaping
at him that the whole story was a lie! "

" I should have told you of the postcard," she said,
with a gesture of annoyance. " It is often just some
such tiny oversight which wrecks a whole plan. One
tries to foresee everything—to provide for everything—and then some little, little detail goes wrong,
and the whole structure comes tumbling down. It
was chance that saved us—but in affairs of this sort,
nothing must be left to chance! If we had failed, it
would have been my fault! "

" But how could there have been a postcard? " demanded Stewart. " I should like to see it."

Smiling, yet with a certain look of anxiety, she
stepped to her bag, took out the postcard, and
handed it to him. On one side was a picture of the
cathedral at Cologne; on the other, the address and
the message:

Cologne, July 31, 1914.

Dear Mary—

Do not forget that it is to-morrow, Saturday, you are to meet me at Aix-la-Chapelle, from where we will go on to Brussels together, as we have planned. If I should fail to meet you at the train, you will find me at a hotel called the Kölner Hof, not far from the station.

With much love,

BRADFORD STEWART.

Stewart read this remarkable message with astonished eyes, then, holding the card close to the candle, he stared at it in bewilderment.

"But it is my handwriting!" he protested. "At least, a fairly good imitation of it—and the signature is mine to a dot."

"Your signature was all the writer had," she explained. "Your handwriting had to be inferred from that."

"Where did you get my signature? Oh, from the blank I filled up at Aix, I suppose. But no," and he looked at the card again, "the postmark shows that it was mailed at Cologne last night."

"The postmark is a fabrication."

"Then it was from the blank at Aix?"

"No," she said, and hesitated, an anxiety in her face he did not understand.

"Then where *did* you get it?" he persisted. "Why shouldn't you tell me?"

" I will tell you," she answered, but her voice was almost inaudible. " It is right that you should know. You gave the signature to the man who examined your passport on the terrace of the Hotel Continental at Cologne, and who recommended you to the Kölner Hof. He also was one of ours."

Stewart was looking at her steadily.

" Then in that case," he said, and his face was gray and stern, " it was I, and no one else, you expected to meet at the Kölner Hof."

" Yes," she answered with trembling lips, but meeting his gaze unwaveringly.

" And all that followed—the tears, the dismay—was make-believe? "

" Yes. I cannot lie to you, my friend."

Stewart passed an unsteady hand before his eyes. It seemed that something had suddenly burst within him—some dream, some vision——

" So I was deliberately used," he began, hoarsely; but she stopped him, her hand upon his arm.

" Do not speak in that tone," she pleaded, her face wrung with anguish. " Do not look at me like that —I did not know—I had never seen you—it was not my plan. We were face to face with failure—we were desperate—there seemed no other way." She stopped, shuddering slightly, and drew away from him. "At least, you will say good-by," she said, softly.

Dazedly Stewart looked at her—at her eyes dark with sadness, at her face suddenly so white——

She was standing near the window, her hand upon the curtain.

"Good-by, my friend," she repeated. "You have been very good to me!"

For an instant longer, Stewart stood staring—then he sprang at her, seized her——

"Do you mean that you are going to leave me?" he demanded, roughly.

"Surely that is what you wish!"

"What I wish? No, no! What do I care—what does it matter!" The words were pouring incoherently from his trembling lips. "I understand— you were desperate—you didn't know me; even if you had, it would make no difference. Don't you understand—nothing can make any difference now!"

She shivered a little; then she drew away, looking at him.

"You mean," she stammered; "you mean that you still—that you still——"

"Little comrade!" he said, and held out his arms.

She lifted her eyes to his—wavered toward him——

"Halt!" cried a voice outside the window, and an instant later there came a heavy hammering on the street door.

CHAPTER IX

THE FRONTIER

THE knocking seemed to shake the house, so violent it was, so insistent; and Stewart, petrified, stood staring numbly. But his companion was quicker than he. In an instant she had run to the light and blown it out. Then she was back at his side.

"The moment they are in the house," she said, "raise the window as silently as you can and unbolt the shutter."

And then she was gone again, and he could hear her moving about near the door.

Again the knocking came, louder than before. It could mean only one thing, Stewart told himself—their ruse had been discovered—a party of soldiers had come to arrest them——

He drew a quick breath. What then? He closed his eyes dizzily—what had she said? "A file of soldiers in front, a wall behind!" But that should never be! They must kill him first! And then he sickened as he realized how puny he was, how utterly powerless to protect her——

He heard shuffling footsteps approach along the
hall, and a glimmer of light showed beneath the
door. For an instant Stewart stared at it uncom-
prehending—then he smiled to himself. The girl,
quicker witted than he, had pulled away the things
that had been stuffed there.

"Who is it?" called the voice of their landlady.

"It is I, Frau Ritter," answered the voice of the
police agent. "Open quickly."

A key rattled in a lock, the door was opened, and
the party stepped inside.

Stewart, at the window, raised the sash and pulled
back the bolt. He could hear the confused murmur
of voices—men's voices——

Then he felt a warm hand in his and lips at his
ear.

"It is the person from Strassburg," she breathed.
"He has been brought here for the night. There is
no danger. Bolt the shutter again—but softly."

She was gone again, and Stewart, with a deep
breath that was almost a sob, thrust home the bolt.
The voices were clearer now—or perhaps it was the
singing of his blood that was stilled—and he could
hear their words.

"You will give this gentleman a room," said the
secret agent.

" Yes, Excellency."

" How are your other guests? "

" I have heard nothing from them, Excellency, since they retired."

Suddenly Stewart felt his hat lifted from his head and a hand rumpling his hair.

" Take off your coat," whispered a voice. " Open the door a little and demand less noise. Say that I am asleep! "

It was a call to battle, and Stewart felt his nerves stiffen. Without a word he threw off his coat and tore off his collar. Then he moved away the chair from before the door, opened it, and put one eye to the crack. There were five people in the hall—the woman, the secret agent, two soldiers, and a man in civilian attire.

" What the deuce is the matter out there? " he demanded.

It did his heart good to see how they jumped at the sound of his voice.

" Your pardon, sir," said the officer, stepping toward him. " I hope we have not disturbed you."

" Disturbed me? Why, I thought you were knocking the house down! "

" Frau Ritter is a heavy sleeper," the other explained with a smile. " You will present my apologies to Madame."

" My wife is so weary that even this has not awakened her, but I hope——"

" What is it, Tommy? " asked a sleepy voice from the darkness behind him. " To whom are you talking out there? "

" Your pardon, madame," said the officer, raising his voice, and doubtless finding a certain piquancy in the situation. " You shall not be disturbed again— I promise it," and he signed for his men to withdraw. " Good-night, sir."

" Good-night! " answered Stewart, and shut the door.

He was so shaken with mirth that he scarcely heard the outer door close. Then he staggered to the bed and collapsed upon it.

" Oh, little comrade! " he gasped. " Little comrade! " and he buried his head in the clothes to choke back the hysterical shouts of laughter which rose in his throat.

" Hush! Hush! " she warned him, her hand on his shoulder. " Get your coat and hat. Be quick! "

The search for those articles of attire sobered him. He had never before realized how large a small room may become in the dark! His coat he found in one corner; his hat miles away in another. His collar and tie seemed to have disappeared utterly, and he was about to abandon them to their fate, when his hand came into contact with them under the bed. He felt utterly exhausted, and sat on the floor panting for breath. Then somebody stumbled against him.

"Where have you been?" her voice demanded impatiently. "What have you been doing?"

"I have been around the world," said Stewart. "And I explored it thoroughly."

Her hand found his shoulder and shook it violently.

"Is this a time for jesting? Come!"

Stewart got heavily to his feet.

"Really," he protested, "I wasn't jesting——"

"Hush!" she cautioned, and suddenly Stewart saw her silhouetted against the window and knew that it was open. Then he saw her peer cautiously out, swing one leg over the sill, and let herself down outside.

"Careful!" she whispered.

In a moment he was standing beside her in the narrow street. She caught his hand and led him away close in the shadow of the wall.

The night air and the movement revived him

somewhat, and by a desperate effort of will he managed to walk without stumbling; but he was still deadly tired. He knew that he was suffering from the reaction from the manifold adventures and excitements of the day, more especially the reaction from despair to hope of the last half hour, and he tried his best to shake it off, marveling at the endurance of this slender girl, who had borne so much more than he.

She went straight on along the narrow street, close in the shadow of the houses, pausing now and then to listen to some distant sound, and once hastily drawing him deep into the shadow of a doorway as a patrol passed along a cross-street.

Then the houses came to an end, and Stewart saw that they were upon a white road running straight away between level fields. Overhead the bright stars shone as calmly and peacefully as though there were no such thing as war in the whole universe, and looking up at them, Stewart felt himself tranquilized and strengthened.

"Now what?" he asked. "I warn you that I shall go to sleep on my feet before long!"

"We must not stop until we are across the frontier. It cannot be farther than half a mile."

Half a mile seemed an eternity to Stewart at that

moment; besides, which way should they go? He gave voice to the question, after a helpless look around, for he had completely lost his bearings.

"Yonder is the Great Bear," said the girl, looking up to where that beautiful constellation stretched brilliantly across the sky. "What is your word for it—the Ladle, is it not?"

"The Dipper," Stewart corrected, reflecting that this was the first time she had been at loss for a word.

"Yes—the Dipper. It will help us to find our way. All I know of astronomy is that a line drawn through the two stars of the bowl points to the North Star. So that insignificant little star up yonder must be the North Star. Now, what is the old formula— if one stands with one's face to the north——"

"Your right hand will be toward the east and your left toward the west," prompted Stewart.

"So the frontier is to our left. Come."

She released his hand, leaped the ditch at the side of the road, and set off westward across a rough field. Stewart stumbled heavily after her; but presently his extreme exhaustion passed, and was followed by a sort of nervous exhilaration which enabled him easily to keep up with her. They climbed a wall, struggled through a strip of woodland—

Stewart had never before realized how difficult it is to go through woods at night!—passed close to a house where a barking dog sent panic terror through them, and came at last to a road running westward, toward Belgium and safety. Along this they hastened as rapidly as they could.

"We must be past the frontier," said Stewart, half an hour later. "We have come at least two miles."

"Let us be sure," gasped the girl. "Let us take no chance!" and she pressed on.

Stewart reflected uneasily that they had encountered no outposts, and surely there would be outposts at the frontier to maintain its neutrality and intercept stragglers; but perhaps that would be only on the main-traveled roads; or perhaps the outposts were not yet in place; or perhaps they might run into one at any moment. He looked forward apprehensively, but the road lay white and empty under the stars.

Suddenly the girl stumbled and nearly fell. His arm was about her in an instant. He could feel how her body drooped against him in utter weariness. She had reached the end of her strength.

"Come," he said; "we must rest," and he led her unresisting to the side of the road.

They sat down close together with their backs
against the wall, and her head for an instant fell
upon his shoulder. By a supreme effort, she roused
herself.

"We cannot stay here!" she protested.

"No," Stewart agreed. "Do you think you can
climb this wall? We may find cover on the other
side."

"Of course I can," and she tried to rise, but
Stewart had to assist her. "I do not know what is
the matter," she panted, as she clung to him. "I
can scarcely stand!"

"It's the reaction," said Stewart. "It was bound
to come, sooner or later. I had my attack back there
on the road. Now I am going to lift you on top of
the wall."

She threw one leg over it and sat astride.

"Oh, I have dropped the bundle," she said.

"Have you been carrying it all this time?"
Stewart demanded.

"Why, of course. It weighs nothing."

Stewart, groping angrily along the base of the
wall, found it, tucked it under his arm, scrambled
over, and lifted her down.

"Now, forward!" he said.

At the second step, they were in a field of grain as

high as their waists. They could feel it brushing against them, twining about their ankles; they could glimpse its yellow expanse stretching away into the night.

"Splendid!" cried Stewart. "There could be no better cover!" and he led her forward into it. "Now," he added, at the end of five minutes, "stand where you are till I get things ready for you," and with his knife he cut down great handfuls of the grain and piled them upon the ground. "There's your bed," he said, placing the bundle of clothing at one end of it; "and there's your pillow."

She sat down with a sigh of relief.

"Oh, how heavenly!"

"You can go to sleep without fear. No one can discover us here, unless they stumble right over us. Good-night, little comrade."

"But you?"

"Oh, I am going to sleep, too. I'll make myself a bed just over here."

"Good-night, my friend!" she said, softly, and Stewart, looking down at her, catching the starry sheen of her uplifted eyes, felt a wild desire to fling himself beside her, to take her in his arms——

Resolutely he turned away and piled his own bed at a little distance. It would have been safer, perhaps, had they slept side by side; but there was about her something delicate and virginal which kept him at a distance—and yet held him too, bound him powerfully, led him captive.

He was filled with the thought of her, as he lay gazing up into the spangled heavens—her beauty, her fire, her indomitable youth, her clear-eyed innocence which left him reverent and trembling. What was her story? Where were her people that they should permit her to take such desperate risks? Why had this great mission been confided to her—to a girl, young, inexperienced? And yet, the choice had evidently been a wise one. She had proved herself worthy of the trust. No one could have been quicker-witted, more ready of resource.

Well, the worst of it was over. They were safe out of Germany. It was only a question now of reaching a farmhouse, of hiring a wagon, of driving to the nearest station——

He stirred uneasily. That would mean good-by. But why should he go to Brussels? Why not turn south with her to France?

Sleep came to him as he was asking himself this question for the twentieth time.

It was full day when he awoke. He looked about for a full minute at the yellow grain, heavy-headed and ready for the harvest, before he remembered where he was. Then he rubbed his eyes and looked again—the wheat-field, certainly—that was all right; but what was that insistent murmur which filled his ears, which never ceased? He sat hastily erect and started to his feet—then as hastily dropped to his knees again and peered cautiously above the grain.

Along the road, as far in either direction as the eye could see, passed a mighty multitude, marching steadily westward. Stewart's heart beat faster as he ran his eyes over that great host—thousands and tens of thousands, clad in greenish-gray, each with his rifle and blanket-roll, his full equipment complete to the smallest detail—the German army setting forth to war! Oh, wonderful, astounding, stupendous!—a myriad of men, moving as one man, obeying one man's bidding, marching out to kill and to be killed.

And marching willingly, even eagerly. The bright morning, the sense of high adventure, the exhilaration of marching elbow to elbow with a thousand comrades—yes, and love of country, the thought that they were fighting for their Fatherland —all these uplifted the heart and made the eye sparkle. Forgotten for the moment were poignant farewells, the tears of women and of children. The round of daily duties, the quiet of the fireside, the circle of familiar faces—all that had receded far into the past. A new life had begun, a larger and more glorious life. They felt that they were men going forward to men's work; they were drinking deep of a cup brimming with the joy of supreme experience!

There were jests and loud laughter; there were snatches of song; and presently a thousand voices were shouting what sounded to Stewart like a mighty hymn—shouting it in slow and solemn unison, marked by the tramp, tramp of their feet. Not until he caught the refrain did he know what it was—"*Deutschland, Deutschland, über alles!*"— the German battle-song, fit expression of the firm conviction that the Fatherland was first, was dearest, must be over all! And as he looked and listened, he felt his own heart thrill responsively, and a new definition of patriotism grouped itself in his mind.

Then suddenly he remembered his companion, and, parting the wheat, he crawled hastily through into the little amphitheater where he had made her bed. She was still asleep, her head pillowed on the bundle of clothing, one arm above her eyes, shielding them from the light. He sat softly down beside her, his heart very tender. She had been so near exhaustion; he must not awaken her——

A blare of bugles shrilled from the road, and from far off rose a roar of cheering, sweeping nearer and nearer.

The girl stirred, turned uneasily, opened her eyes, stared up at him for a moment, and then sat hastily erect.

" What is it? " she asked.

" The German army is advancing."

" Yes—but the cheering? "

" I don't know."

Side by side, they peered out above the grain. A heavy motor-car was advancing rapidly from the east along the road, the troops drawing aside to let it pass, and cheering—cheering, as though mad.

Inside the car were three men, but the one who acknowledged the salutes of the officers as he passed was a tall, slender young fellow in a long, gray coat. His face was radiant, and he saluted and saluted, and once or twice rose to his feet and pointed westward.

" The Crown Prince! " said the girl, and watched in heavy silence until the motor passed from sight and the host took up its steady march again. " Ah, well, he at least has realized his ambition—to lead an army against France!"

"It seems to be a devoted army," Stewart remarked. "I never heard such cheering."

"It is a splendid army," and the girl swept her eyes back and forth over the marching host. "France will have no easy task—but she is fighting for her life, and she will win!"

"I hope so," Stewart agreed; but his heart misgave him as he looked at these marching men, sweeping on endlessly, irresistibly, in a torrent which seemed powerful enough to engulf everything in its path.

He had never before seen an army, even a small one, and this mighty host unnerved and intimidated him. It was so full of vigor, so self-confident, so evidently certain of victory! It was so sturdy, so erect, so proud! There was about it an electric sense of power; it almost strutted as it marched!

"There is one thing certain," he said, at last, "and that is that our adventures are not yet over. With our flight discovered, and Germans in front of us and behind us and probably on either side of us, our position is still decidedly awkward. I suppose their outposts are somewhere ahead."

"Yes, I suppose so," she agreed. "Along the Meuse, perhaps."

"And I am most awfully hungry. Aren't you?"

"Yes, I am."

"I have heard that whole wheat makes a delicious breakfast dish," said Stewart, who felt unaccountably down-hearted and was determined not to show it. "Shall we try some?"

She nodded, smiling, then turned back to watch the Germans, as though fascinated by them. Stewart broke off a dozen heads of yellow grain, rubbed them out between his hands, blew away the chaff, and poured the fat kernels into her outstretched palm. Then he rubbed out a mouthful for himself.

"But that they should invade Belgium!" she said, half to herself. "Did you hear what that man said last night—that a treaty was only a scrap of paper—that if Belgium resisted, she would be crushed?"

"Yes," nodded Stewart, "and it disgusted me!"

"But of course France has expected it—she has prepared for it!" went on the girl, perhaps to silence her own misgivings. "She will not be taken by surprise!"

"You don't think, then, that the Kaiser will dine in Paris on the twelfth?"

"Nonsense—that was only an empty boast!"

"Well, I hope so," said Stewart. "And wherever he dines, I hope that he has something more appetizing than whole wheat *au naturel*. I move we look for a house and try to get some real food that we can put our teeth into. Also something to drink."

"Yes, we must be getting forward," she agreed.

Together they peered out again above the grain. The massed column was still passing, shimmering along the dusty road like a mighty green-gray serpent.

"Isn't there any end to these fellows?" Stewart asked. "We must have seen about a million!"

"Oh, no; this is but a single division—and there are at least a hundred divisions in the German army! No doubt there is another division on each of the roads leading into Belgium. We shall have to keep away from the roads. Let us work our way back through the grain to that strip of woodland. No," she added, as Stewart stooped to pick up the bundle of clothing, "we must leave that. If we should happen to be stopped, it would betray us. What are you doing?"

Without replying, Stewart opened the bundle, thoughtfully selected a strand of the beautiful hair inside it and placed the lock carefully in a flapped

compartment of his pocket-book. Then he re-tied
the bundle and threw over it some of the severed
stalks.

"It seems a shame to leave it," he said. "That
is a beautiful gown—and the hair! Think of those
barbarians opening the bundle and finding that lovely
hair!"

The girl, who had been watching him with brilliant eyes, laughed a little and caught his hand.

"How foolish! Come along! I think I shall let
you keep that lock of hair!" she added, thoughtfully.

Stewart looked at her quickly and saw that the
dimple was visible.

"Thank you!" he said. "Of course I should
have asked. Forgive me!"

She gave him a flashing little smile, then, bending
low, hurried forward through the grain. Beyond
the field lay a stretch of woodland, and presently they
heard the sound of running water, and came to a
brook flowing gently over a clean and rocky bed.

With a cry of delight, the girl dropped to her
knees beside it, bent far over and drank deep; then
threw off her coat, pushed her sleeves above her
elbows, and laved hands and face in the cool water.

"How fortunate my hair is short!" she said, contemplating her reflection. " Otherwise it would be a perfect tangle. I make a very nice boy, do you not think so ? "

" An adorable boy ! " agreed Stewart, heartily.

She glanced up at him.

" Thank you ! But are you not going to wash ? "

" Not until you have finished. You are such a radiant beauty, that it would be a sin to miss an instant of you. My clothes are even more becoming to you than your own ! "

She glanced down over her slender figure, so fine, so delicately rounded, then sprang quickly to her feet and snatched up the coat.

" I will reconnoiter our position while you make your toilet," she said, and slipped out of sight among the trees.

Ten minutes later, Stewart found her seated on a little knoll at the edge of the wood, looking out across the country.

" There is a house over yonder," she said, nodding to where the corner of a gable showed among the trees. " But it may be dangerous to approach it."

" We can't starve," he pointed out. " And we seem to be lucky. Suppose I go on ahead ? "

" No; we will go together," and she sprang to her feet.

The way led over a strip of rocky ground, used evidently as a pasture, but there were no cattle grazing on it; then along a narrow lane between low stone walls. Presently they reached the house, which seemed to be the home of a small farmer, for it stood at the back of a yard with stables and sheds grouped about it. The gate was open and there was no sign of life within. Stewart started to enter, but suddenly stopped and looked at his companion.

"There is something wrong here," he said, almost in a whisper. "I feel it."

"So do I," said the girl, and stared about at the deserted space, shivering slightly. Then she looked upward into the clear sky. "It was as if a cloud had come between me and the sun," she added.

"Perhaps it is just that everything seems so deserted," said Stewart, and stepped through the gate.

"No doubt the people fled when they saw the Germans," she suggested; "or perhaps it was just a rumor that frightened them away."

Stewart looked about him. It was not only people that were missing from this farmyard, he told himself; there should have been pigs in the sty, chickens scratching in the straw, pigeons on the roof, a cat on the door-step.

"We must have food," he said, and went forward resolutely to the door, which stood ajar.

There was something vaguely sinister in the position of the door, half-open and half-closed, but after an instant's hesitation, he knocked loudly. A minute passed, and another, and there was no response. Nerving himself as though for a mighty effort, he pushed the door open and looked into the room beyond.

It was evidently the living-room and dining-room combined, and it was in the wildest disorder. Chairs were overturned, a table was lying on its side with one leg broken, dishes lay smashed upon the floor.

Summoning all his resolution, Stewart stepped inside. What frightful thing had happened here? From the chairs and the dishes, it looked as if the family had been surprised at breakfast. But where was the family? Who had surprised them? What had——

And then his heart leaped sickeningly as his eyes fell upon a huddled figure lying in one corner, close against the wall. It was the body of a woman, her clothing disordered, a long, gleaming bread-knife clutched tightly in one hand; and as Stewart bent above her, he saw that her head had been beaten in.

CHAPTER X

FORTUNE FROWNS

ONE look at that disfigured countenance imprinted it indelibly on Stewart's memory—the blue eyes staring horribly upward from under the shattered forehead, the hair matted with blood, the sprawling body, the gleaming knife caught up in what moment of desperation! Shaking with horror, he seized his companion's hand and led her away out of the desecrated house, out of the silent yard, out into the narrow lane where they could breathe freely.

"The Uhlans have passed this way," said the girl, staring up and down the road.

"But," stammered Stewart, wiping his wet forehead, "but I don't understand. Germany is a civilized nation—war is no longer the brutal thing it once was."

"War is always brutal, I fear," said the girl, sadly; "and of course, among a million men, there are certain to be some—like that! I am no longer hungry. Let us press on."

Stewart, nodding, followed along beside her, across fields, over little streams, up and down stretches of rocky hillside, always westward. But he saw nothing; his mind was full of other things— of the gray-clad thousands singing as they marched; of the radiant face of the Crown Prince; of that poor murdered woman, who had risen happily this Sunday morning, glad of a day of rest, and looked up to see strange faces at the door——

And this was war. A thousand other women would suffer the same fate; thousands and thousands more would be thrown stripped and defenseless on the world, to live or die as chance might will; a hundred thousand children would be fatherless; a hundred thousand girls, now ripening into womanhood, would be denied their rightful destiny of marriage and children of their own——

Stewart shook the thought away. The picture his imagination painted was too horrible; it could never come true—not all the emperors on earth could make it come true!

He looked about him at the mellow landscape. Nowhere was there a sign of life. The yellow wheat stood ripe for the harvest. The pastures stretched lush and green—and empty. Here and there above the trees he caught a glimpse of farm-house chimneys, but no reassuring smoke floated above them. A peaceful land, truly, so he told himself—peaceful as death!

Gradually the country grew rougher and more broken, and ahead of them they could see steep and rocky hillsides, cleft by deep valleys and covered by a thick growth of pine.

"We must find a road," said Stewart at last; "we can't climb up and down those hills. And we must find out where we are. There is a certain risk, but we must take it. It is foolish to stumble forward blindly."

"You are right," his companion agreed, and when presently, far below them at the bottom of a valley, they saw a white road winding, they made their way down to it. Almost at once they came to a house, in whose door stood a buxom, fair-haired woman, with a child clinging to her skirts.

The woman watched them curiously as they approached, and her face seemed to Stewart distinctly friendly.

"Good-morning," he said, stopping before the door-step and lifting his hat—an unaccustomed salutation at which the woman stared. "We seem to have lost our way. Can you tell us——"

The woman shook her head.

"My brother and I have lost our way," said his companion, in rapid French. "We have been tramping the hills all morning. How far is it to the nearest village?"

"The nearest village is Battice," answered the woman in the same language. "It is three kilometers from here."

"Has it a railway station?"

"But certainly. How is it you do not know?"

"We come from the other direction."

"From Germany?"

"Yes," answered the girl, after an instant's scrutiny of the woman's face.

"Then you are fugitives? Ah, do not fear to tell me," she added, as the girl hesitated. "I have no love for the Germans. I have lived near them too long!"

There could be no doubting the sincerity of the words, nor the grimace of disgust which accompanied them.

"Yes," assented the girl, "we are fugitives. We are trying to get to Liège. Have the Germans been this way?"

"No; I have seen nothing of them, but I have heard that a great army has passed along the road through Verviers."

"Where is your man?"

"He has joined the army, as have all the men in this neighborhood."

"The German army?"

"Oh, no; the Belgian army. It is doing what it can to hold back the Germans."

The girl's face lighted with enthusiasm.

"Oh, how splendid!" she cried. "How splendid for your brave little country to defy the invader! Bravo, Belgium!"

The woman smiled at her enthusiasm, but shook her head doubtfully.

"I do not know," she said, simply. "I do not understand these things. I only know that my man has gone, and that I must harvest our grain and cut our winter wood by myself. But will you not enter and rest yourselves?"

"Thank you. And we are very hungry. We have money to pay for food, if you can let us have some."

"Certainly, certainly," and the good wife bustled before them into the house.

An hour later, rested, refreshed, with a supply of sandwiches in their pockets, and armed with a rough map drawn from the directions of their hostess, they were ready to set out westward again. She was of the opinion that they could pass safely through Battice, which was off the main road of the German advance, and that they might even secure there a vehicle of some sort to take them onward. The trains, she understood, were no longer running. Finally they thanked her for the twentieth time and bade her good-by. She wished them Godspeed, and stood watching them from the door until they disappeared from view.

They pushed forward briskly, and presently, huddled in the valley below them, caught sight of the gabled roofs of the village. A bell was ringing vigorously, and they could see the people—women and children for the most part—gathering in toward the little church, crowned by its gilded cross. Evidently nothing had occurred to disturb the serenity of Battice.

Reassured, the two were about to push on down the road, when suddenly, topping the opposite slope, they saw a squadron of horsemen, perhaps fifty strong. They were clad in greenish-gray, and each of them bore upright at his right elbow a long lance.

"Uhlans!" cried the girl, and the fugitives stopped short, watching with bated breath.

The troop swung down the road toward the village at a sharp trot, and presently Stewart could distinguish their queer, flat-topped helmets, reminding him of the mortar-board of his university days. Right at the edge of the village, in the shadow of some trees, the horsemen drew rein and waited until the bell ceased ringing and the last of the congregation had entered the church; then, at the word of command, they touched spur to flank and swept through the empty street.

A boy saw them first and raised a shout of alarm; then a woman, hurrying toward the church, heard the clatter of hoofs, cast one glance behind her, and ran on, screaming wildly. The screams penetrated the church, and in a moment the congregation came pouring out, only to find themselves hemmed in by a semicircle of lowered lances.

The lieutenant shouted a command, and four of his men threw themselves from the saddle and disappeared into the church. They were back in a moment, dragging between them a white-haired priest clad in stole and surplice, and a rosy-faced old man, who, even in this trying situation, managed to retain his dignity.

The two were placed before the officer, and a short conference followed, with the townspeople pressing anxiously around, listening to every word. Suddenly there was an outburst of protest and despair, which the priest quieted with a motion of his hand, and the conference was resumed.

"What is it the fellow wants?" asked Stewart.

"Money and supplies, I suppose."

"Money and supplies? But that's robbery!"

"Oh, no; it is a part of the plan of the German General Staff. How many times have I heard Prussian officers boast that a war would cost Germany nothing—that her enemies would be made to bear the whole burden! It has all been arranged—the indemnity which each village, even the smallest, must pay—the amount of supplies which each must furnish, the ransom which will be assessed on each individual. This lieutenant of Uhlans is merely carrying out his instructions!"

"Who is the old man?"

"The burgomaster, doubtless. He and the priest are always the most influential men in a village."

The conference was waxing warmer, the lieutenant was talking in a loud voice, and once he shook his fist menacingly; again there was a wail of protest from the crowd—women were wringing their hands——

"He is demanding more than the village can supply," remarked the girl. "That is not surprising," she added, with a bitter smile. "They will always demand more than can be supplied. But come; we must be getting on."

Stewart would have liked to see the end of the drama, but he followed his companion over the wall at the side of the road, and then around the village and along the rough hillside. Suddenly from the houses below arose a hideous tumult—shouts, curses, the smashing of glass—and in a moment, a flood of people, wailing, screaming, shaking their fists in the air, burst from the town and swept along the road in the direction of Herve.

" They would better have given all that was demanded," said the girl, looking down at them. " Now they will be made to serve as an example to other villages—they will lose everything—even their houses—see ! "

Following the direction of her pointing finger, Stewart saw a black cloud of smoke bulging up from one end of the village.

" But surely," he gasped, " they're not burning it ! They wouldn't dare do that ! "

" Why not ? "

" Isn't looting prohibited by the rules of war ? "

" Certainly—looting and the destruction of property of non-combatants."

" Well, then——"

But he stopped, staring helplessly. The cloud of smoke grew in volume, and below it could be seen red tongues of flame. There before him was the hideous reality—and he suddenly realized how futile it was to make laws for anything so essentially lawless as war, or to expect niceties of conduct from men thrown back into a state of barbarism.

"What do the rules of war matter to a nation which considers treaties mere scraps of paper?" asked the girl, in a hard voice. "Their very presence here in Belgium is a violation of the rules of war. Besides, it is the German theory that war should be ruthless—that the enemy must be intimidated, ravaged, despoiled in every possible way. They say that the more merciless it is, the briefer it will be. It is possible that they are not altogether wrong."

"True," muttered Stewart. "But it is a heartless theory."

"War is a heartless thing," commented his companion, turning away. "It is best not to think too much about it. Come—we must be going on."

They pushed forward again, keeping the road, with its rabble of frenzied fugitives, at their right. It was a wild and beautiful country, and under other circumstances, Stewart would have gazed in admiring wonder at its rugged cliffs, its deep precipitous valleys, its thickly-wooded hillsides; but now these appeared to him only as so many obstacles between him and safety.

At last the valley opened out, and below them they saw the clustered roofs of another village, which could only be Herve. Around it were broad pastures and fields of yellow grain, and suddenly the girl caught Stewart by the arm.

"Look!" she said, and pointed to the field lying nearest them.

A number of old men, women, and children were cutting the grain, tying it into sheaves, and piling the sheaves into stacks, under the supervision of four men. Those four men were clothed in greenish-gray and carried rifles in their hands! The invaders were stripping the grain from the fields in order to feed their army!

As he contemplated this scene, Stewart felt, mixed with his horror and detestation, a sort of unwilling admiration. Evidently, as his companion had said, when Germany made war, she made war. She was ruthlessly thorough. She allowed no sentiment, no feeling of pity, no weakening compassion, to inter-fere between her and her goal. She went to war with but one purpose: to win; and she was determined to win, no matter what the cost! Stewart shivered at the thought. Whether she won or lost, how awful that cost must be!

The fugitives went on again at last, working their way around the village, keeping always in the shelter of the woods along the hillsides, and after a weary journey, came out on the other side above the line of the railroad. A sentry, with fixed bayonet, stood guard over a solitary engine; except for him, the road seemed quite deserted. For half a mile they toiled along over the rough hillside above it without seeing anyone else.

"We can't keep this up," said Stewart, flinging himself upon the ground. "We shall have to take to the road if we are to make any progress. Do you think we'd better risk it?"

"Let us watch it for a while," the girl suggested, so they sat and watched it and munched their sandwiches, and talked in broken snatches. Ten minutes passed, but no one came in sight.

"It seems quite safe," she said at last, and together they made their way down to it.

"The next village is Fléron," said Stewart, consulting his rough map. "It is apparently about four miles from here. Liège is about ten miles further. Can we make it to-night?"

"We must!" said the girl, fiercely. "Come!"

The road descended steadily along the valley of a pretty river, closed in on either side by densely-wooded hills. Here and there among the trees, they caught glimpses of white villas; below them, along the river, there was an occasional cluster of houses; but they saw few people. Either the inhabitants of this land had fled before the enemy, or were keeping carefully indoors out of his way.

Once the fugitives had an alarm, for a hand-car, manned by a squad of German soldiers, came spinning past; but fortunately Stewart heard it singing along the rails in time to pull his companion into a clump of underbrush. A little later, along the highway by the river, they saw a patrol of Uhlans riding, and then they came to Fléron and took to the hills to pass around it. Here, too, clouds of black smoke hung heavy above certain of the houses, which, for some reason, had been made the marks of German reprisals; and once, above the trees to their right, they saw a column of smoke drifting upward, marking the destruction of some isolated dwelling.

The sun was sinking toward the west by the time they again reached the railroad, and they were both desperately weary; but neither had any thought of rest. The shadows deepened rapidly among the hills, but the darkness was welcome, for it meant added safety. By the time they reached Bois de Breux, night had come in earnest, so they made only a short détour, and were soon back on the railroad again, with scarcely five miles to go. For an hour longer they plodded on through the darkness, snatching a few minutes' rest once or twice; too weary to talk, or to look to right or left.

Then, as they turned a bend in the road, they drew back in alarm; for just ahead of them, close beside the track, a bright fire was burning, lighting up the black entrance of a tunnel, before which stood a sentry leaning on his rifle. Five or six other soldiers, wearing flat fatigue caps, were lolling about the fire, smoking and talking in low tones.

Stewart surveyed them curiously. They were big, good-humored-looking fellows, fathers of families doubtless—honest men with kindly hearts. It seemed absurd to suppose that such men as these would loot villages and burn houses and outrage women; it seemed absurd that anyone should fear them or hide from them. Stewart, with a feeling that all this threat of war was a chimera, had an impulse to go forward boldly and join them beside the fire. He was sure they would welcome him, make a place for him——

" *Wer da?* " called, sharply, a voice behind him, and he spun around to find himself facing a leveled rifle, behind which he could see dimly the face of a man wearing a spiked helmet—a patrol, no doubt, who had seen them as they stood carelessly outlined against the fire, and who had crept upon them unheard.

" We are friends," Stewart answered, hastily.

The soldier motioned them forward to the fire. The men there had caught up their rifles at the sound of the challenge, and stood peering anxiously out into the darkness. But when the two captives came within the circle of light cast by the fire, they stacked their guns and sat down again. Evidently they saw nothing threatening in the appearance of either Stewart or his companion.

Their captor added his gun to the stack and motioned them to sit down. Then he doffed his heavy helmet with evident relief and hung it on his rifle, got out a soft cap like the others', and finally sat down opposite his prisoners and looked at them closely.

" What are you doing here? " he demanded in German.

" We are trying to get through to Brussels," answered Stewart, in the best German he could muster.

"I have not much German. Do you speak English?"

"No. Are you English?" And the blue eyes glinted with an unfriendly light which Stewart was at a loss to understand.

"We are Americans," and Stewart saw with relief that the man's face softened perceptibly. On the chance that, if the soldier could not speak English, neither could he read it, he impressively produced his passport. "Here is our safe-conduct from our Secretary of State," he said. "You will see that it is sealed with the seal of the United States. My brother and I were passed at Herbesthal, but could find no conveyance and started to walk. We lost our way, but stumbled upon the railroad some miles back and decided to follow it until we came to a village. How far away is the nearest village?"

"I do not know," said the man, curtly; but he took the passport and stared at it curiously. Then he passed it around the circle, and it finally came back to its owner, who placed it in his pocket.

"You find it correct?" Stewart inquired.

"I know nothing about it. You must wait until our officer arrives."

Stewart felt a sickening sensation at his heart, but he managed to smile.

"He will not be long, I hope," he said. "We are very tired and hungry."

"He will not be long," answered the other, shortly, and got out a long pipe, but Stewart stopped him with a gesture.

"Try one of these," he said, quickly, and brought out his handful of cigars and passed them around.

The men grinned their thanks, and were soon puffing away with evident enjoyment. But to Stewart the single cigar he had kept for himself seemed strangely savorless. He glanced at his companion. She was sitting hunched up, her arms about her knees, staring thoughtfully at the fire.

"This man says we must wait here until their officer arrives," he explained in English. "My brother does not understand German," he added to the men.

"How stupid!" said the girl. "I am so tired and stiff!"

"It is no use to argue with them, I suppose?"

"No. They will refuse to decide anything for themselves. They rely wholly upon their officers."

She rose wearily, stretched herself, stamped her foot as if it were asleep, and then sat down again and closed her eyes. She looked very young and fragile, and was shivering from head to foot.

"My brother is not strong," said Stewart to the attentive group. "I fear all this hardship and exposure will be more than he can bear."

One of the men, with a gesture of sympathy, rose, unrolled his blanket, and spread it on the bank behind the fire.

"Let the young man lie down there," he said.

"Oh, thank you!" cried Stewart. "Come, Tommy," he added, touching the girl on the arm. "Suppose you lie down till the officer comes."

She opened her eyes, saw the blanket, nodded sleepily, and, still shivering, followed Stewart to it, lay down, permitted him to roll her in it, and apparently dropped off to sleep on the instant. Stewart returned to the circle about the fire, nodding his satisfaction. They all smiled, as men do who have performed a kind action.

But Stewart, though doing his best to keep a placid countenance, was far from easy in his mind. One thing was certain—they must escape before the officer arrived. He, no doubt, would be able both to read and speak English, and the passport would betray them at once. For without question, a warning had been flashed from headquarters to every patrol to arrest the holder of that passport, and to send him and his companion, under close guard, back to Herbesthal. But how to escape!

Stewart glanced carefully about him, cursing the carelessness that had brought them into this trap, the imbecility which had held them staring at this outpost, instead of taking instantly to the woods, as they should have done. They deserved to be captured! Nevertheless——

The sentry was pacing slowly back and forth at the tunnel entrance, fifteen yards away; the other men were lolling about the fire, half-asleep. It would be possible, doubtless, to bolt into the darkness before they could grab their rifles, so there was only the sentry to fear, and the danger from him would not be very great. But it would be necessary to keep to the track for some distance, because, where it dropped into the tunnel, its sides were precipices impossible to scale in the darkness. The danger, then, lay in the fact that the men might have time to snatch up their rifles and empty them along the track before the fugitives would be able to leave it. But it was a danger which must be faced—there was no other way. Once in the woods, they would be safe.

Stewart, musing over the situation with eyes half-closed, recalled dim memories of daring escapes from Indians and outlaws, described in detail in the blood-and-thunder reading of his youth. There was always one ruse which never failed—just as the pursuers were about to fire, the fugitive would fling himself flat on his face, and the bullets would fly harmlessly over him; then he would spring to his feet and go safely on his way. Stewart smiled to remember how religiously he had believed in that stratagem, and how he had determined to practice it, if ever need arose! He had never contemplated the possibility of having to flee from a squad of men armed with magazine rifles, capable of firing twenty-five shots a minute!

Then he shook these thoughts away; there was no time to be lost. He must warn his companion, for they must make the dash at the same instant. He glanced toward where she lay in the shadow of the cliff, and saw that she was turning restlessly from side to side, as though fevered. With real anxiety, he hastened to her, knelt beside her, and placed his hand gently on her forehead. At the touch, she opened her eyes and stared dazedly up at him.

"Ask for some water," she said, weakly; and then, in the same tone, "we must flee at the moment they salute their officer."

Stewart turned to the soldiers, who were listening with inquiring faces.

"My brother is feverish," he explained. "He asks for a drink of water."

One of the men was instantly on his feet, unscrewing his canteen and holding it to the eager lips while Stewart supported his comrade's head. She drank eagerly and then dropped back with a sigh of satisfaction, and closed her eyes.

"He will go to sleep now," said Stewart. "Thank you," and he himself took a drink from the proffered flask.

He was surprised to find how cool and fresh the water tasted, and when he looked at the flask more closely, he saw that it was made like a Thermos bottle, with outer and inner shells. He handed it back to its owner with a nod of admiration.

"That is very clever," he said. "Everything seems to have been thought of."

"Yes, everything," agreed the other. "No army is equipped like ours. I am told that the French are in rags."

"I don't know," said Stewart, cautiously, "I have never seen them."

"And their army is not organized; we shall be in Paris before they can mobilize. It will be 1870 over again. The war will be ended in two or three months. It has been promised us that we shall be home again for Christmas without fail."

"I hope you will," Stewart agreed; and there was a moment's silence. "How much longer shall we have to wait?" he asked, at last.

"Our officer should be here at any moment."

"It is absolutely necessary that we wait for him?"

"Yes, absolutely."

"We are very hungry," Stewart explained.

The soldier pondered for a moment, and then rose to his feet.

"I think I can give you food," he said. "It is permitted to give food, is it not?" he asked his comrades; and when they nodded, he opened his knapsack and took out a package of hard, square biscuits and a thick roll of sausage. He cut the sausage into generous slices, while Stewart watched with watering mouth, placed a slice on each of the biscuits, and passed them over.

"Splendid!" cried Stewart. "I don't know how to thank you. But at least I can pay you," and he dove into his pocket and produced a ten-mark piece —his last. The soldier shook his head. "It is for the whole squad," added Stewart, persuasively.

"You will be needing tobacco some day, and this will come in handy!"

The soldier smiled, took the little coin, and placed it carefully in his pocket.

"You are right about the tobacco," he said. "I thank you."

He sat down again before the fire, while Stewart hastened to his companion and dropped to his knees beside her.

"See what I've got!" he cried. "Food!"

She opened her eyes, struggled to a sitting posture, and held out an eager hand. A moment later, they were both munching the sausage and biscuits as though they had never tasted anything so delicious— as, indeed, they never had!

"Oh, how good that was!" she said, when the last crumb was swallowed, and she waved her thanks to the watching group about the fire. "Remember," she added, in a lower tone, as she sank back upon her elbow, "the instant——"

She stopped, staring toward the tunnel, one hand grasping the blanket.

Stewart, following her look, saw the sentry stiffen, turn on his heel, and hold his rifle rigidly in front of him, as a tall figure, clad in a long gray coat and carrying an electric torch, stepped out of the darkness of the tunnel. At the same instant, the men about the fire sprang to their feet.

" Now!" cried the girl, and threw back the blanket.

In an instant, hand in hand, they had glided into the darkness.

CHAPTER XI

THE NIGHT ATTACK

A savage voice behind them shouted, "Halt!" and then a bullet sang past and a rifle went off with a noise like a cannon—or so it seemed to Stewart; then another and another. It was the sentry, of course, pumping bullets after them. Stewart's flesh crept at the thought that any instant might bring a volley, which would sweep the track with a storm of lead. If he could only look back, if he only knew——

Suddenly the girl pulled him to the right, and he saw there was a cleft in the steep bank. Even as they sprang into it, the volley came, and then a second and a third, and then the sound of shouting voices and running feet.

Savagely the fugitives fought their way upward, over rocks, through briars—scratched, torn, bleeding, panting for breath. Even in the daytime it would have been a desperate scramble; now it soon became a sort of horrid nightmare, which might end at any instant at the bottom of a cliff. More than once Stewart told himself that he could not go on, that his heart would burst if he took another step—and yet he *did* go on, up and up, close behind his comrade, who seemed borne on invisible wings.

At last she stopped and pressed close against him. He could feel how her heart was thumping.

"Wait!" she panted. "Listen!"

Not a sound broke the stillness of the wood.

"I think we are safe," she said. "Let us rest a while."

They sat down, side by side, on a great rock. Gradually their gasping breath slackened and the pounding of their hearts grew quieter.

"I have lost my cap," she said, at last. "A branch snatched it off and I did not dare to stop."

Stewart put his hand to his head and found that his hat also was gone. Until that instant he had not missed it.

"I feel as if I had been flayed," he said. "Those briars were downright savage. It was lucky we didn't break a leg—or stop a bullet."

"We must not run such risks again. We must keep clear of roads—the Germans seem to be everywhere. Let us keep on until we reach the crest of this hill, and then we can rest till daylight."

"All right," agreed Stewart. "Where thou goest, I will go. But please remember I don't travel on angelic wings as you do, but on very human legs! And they are very tired!"

"So are mine!" she laughed. "But we cannot remain here, can we?"

"No," said Stewart, "I suppose not," and he arose and followed her.

The ground grew less rough as they proceeded, and at last they came to the end of the wood. Overhead, a full moon was sinking toward the west—a moon which lighted every rock and crevice of the rolling meadow before them, and which seemed to them, after the darkness of the woods and the valleys, as brilliant as the sun.

"We must be nearly at the top," said the girl. "These hills almost all have meadows on their summits where the peasants pasture their flocks."

And so it proved, for beyond the meadow was another narrow strip of woodland, and as they came to its farther edge, the fugitives stopped with a gasp of astonishment.

Below them stretched a broad valley, and as far as the eye could reach, it was dotted with flaring fires.

"The German army!" said the girl, and the two stood staring.

Evidently a countless host lay camped below them, but no sound reached them, save the occasional rumble of a train along some distant track. The Kaiser's legions were sleeping until the dawn should give the signal for the advance—an advance which would be as the sweep of an avalanche, hideous, irresistible, remorseless, crushing everything in its path.

"Oh, look, look!" cried the girl, and caught him by the arm.

To the west, seemingly quite near, a flash of flame gleamed against the sky, then another and another and another, and in a moment a savage rumble as of distant thunder drifted to their ears.

"What is it?" asked Stewart, staring at the ever-increasing bursts of flame. "Not a battle, surely!"

"It is the forts at Liège!" cried the girl, hoarsely. "The Germans are attacking them, and they resist! Oh, brave little Belgium!"

The firing grew more furious, and then a battery of searchlights began to play over the hillside before the nearest fort, and they could dimly see its outline on the hilltop—strangely like a dreadnaught, with its wireless mast and its armored turrets vomiting flame. Above it, from time to time, a shell from the German batteries burst like a greenish-white rocket, but it was evident that the assailants had not yet got their guns up in any number.

Then, suddenly, amid the thunder of the cannon, there surged a vicious undercurrent of sound which Stewart knew must be the reports of machine-guns, or perhaps of rifles; and all along the slope below the fort innumerable little flashes stabbed upward toward the summit. Surely infantry would never attack such a position, Stewart told himself; and then he held his breath, for, full in the glare of the searchlights, he could see what seemed to be a tidal wave sweeping up the hill.

A very fury of firing came from the fort, yet still the wave swept on. As it neared the fort, what seemed to be another wave swept down to meet it. The firing slackened, almost stopped, and Stewart, his blood pounding in his temples, knew that the struggle was hand to hand, breast to breast. It lasted but a minute; then the attacking tide flowed back down the hill, and again the machine-guns of the fort took up that deadly chorus.

" They have been driven back! " gasped the girl. "Thank God! the Germans have been driven back! "

How many, Stewart wondered, were lying out there dead on the hillside? How many homes had been rendered fatherless in those few desperate moments? And this was but the first of a thousand such charges—the first of a thousand such moments! There, before his eyes, men had killed each other—for what? The men in the forts were defending their Fatherland from invasion—they were fighting for liberty and independence. That was understandable—it was even admirable. But those others—the men in the spiked helmets—what were they fighting for? To destroy liberty? To wrest independence from a proud little people? Surely no man of honor would fight for that! No, it must be for something else—for some ideal—for some ardent sense of duty, strangely twisted, perhaps, but none the less fierce and urgent!

Again the big guns in the armored turrets were bellowing forth their wrath; and then the searchlights stabbed suddenly up into the sky, sweeping this way and that.

"They fear an airship attack!" breathed the girl, and she and Stewart stood staring up into the night.

Shells from the German guns began again to burst about the fort, but its own guns were silent, and it lay there crouching as if in terror. Only its searchlights swept back and forth.

Suddenly a gun spoke—they could see the flash of its discharge, seemingly straight up into the air; then a second and a third; and then the searchlights caught the great bulk of a Zeppelin and held it clearly outlined as it swept across the sky. There was a furious burst of firing, but the ship sped on unharmed, passed beyond the range of the searchlights, blotted out the setting moon for an instant, and was gone.

" It did not dare pass over the fort," said the girl. " It was flying too low. Perhaps it will come back at a greater altitude. I have seen them at the maneuvers in Alsace—frightful things, moving like the wind."

This way and that the searchlights swept in great arcs across the heavens, in frenzied search for this monster of the air; but it did not return. Perhaps it had been damaged by the gunfire—or perhaps, Stewart told himself with a shiver, it was speeding on toward Paris, to rain terror from the August sky!

Gradually the firing ceased; but the more distant forts were using their searchlights, too. Seeing them all aroused and vigilant, the Germans did not attack again; their surprise had failed; now they must wait for their heavy guns.

" Well," asked Stewart, at last, " what now? "

" I think it would be well to stay here till morning—then we can see how the army is placed and how best to get past it. It is evident we cannot go on to-night."

" I'm deadly tired," said Stewart, looking about him into the darkness, " but I should like a softer bed than the bare ground."

" Let us go to the edge of this meadow," the girl suggested. " Perhaps we shall find another field of grain."

But luck was against them. Beyond the meadow the woods began again.

" The meadow is better than the woods," said Stewart. " At least it has some grass on it—the woods have nothing but rocks! "

" Let us stay in the shelter of the hedge. Then, if a patrol happens into the field before we are awake, it will not see us. Perhaps they will attempt a pursuit in the morning. They will guess that we have headed for the west."

" I don't think there's much danger—it would be like hunting for a needle in a haystack—in a dozen haystacks! But won't you be cold? "

" Oh, no," she protested, quickly; " the night is quite warm. Good-night, my friend."

" Good-night," Stewart answered, and withdrew a few steps and made himself as comfortable as he could.

There were irritating bumps in the ground which seemed to come exactly in the wrong place; but he finally adjusted himself, and lay and looked up at the stars, and wondered what the morrow would bring forth. He was growing a little weary of the adventure. He was growing weary of the restraint which the situation imposed upon him. He was aching to take this girl in his arms and hold her close, and whisper three words—just three!—into her rosy ear—but to do that now, to do it until they were in safety, until she had no further need of him, would be a cowardly thing—a cowardly thing —a cowardly——

He was awakened by a touch on the arm, and opened his eyes to find the sun high in the heavens and his comrade looking down at him with face almost equally radiant.

" I did not like to wake you," she said, " but it is getting late."

Stewart sat up and rubbed his eyes and looked at her again. Her hair was neatly combed, her face was fresh and shining, her hands showed some ugly scratches but were scrupulously clean. Even her clothing, though torn here and there, had evidently been carefully brushed.

"What astounds me," said Stewart, deliberately, "is how you do it. You spend the first half of the night scrambling over rocks and through briars, and the second half sleeping on the bare ground, and you emerge in the morning as fresh and radiant as though you had just stepped from your boudoir. I wish I knew the secret."

"Come and I will show you," she said, laughing gayly, and she led him away into the wood.

Presently he heard the sound of falling water, and his guide brought him triumphantly to a brook gurgling over mossy rocks, at whose foot was a shallow basin.

"There is my boudoir," she said. "The secret of beauty is in the bath. I will reconnoiter the neighborhood while you try it for yourself."

Stewart flung off his clothes, splashed joyously into the cold, clear water, and had perhaps the most delicious bath of his life. There was no soap, to be sure, but much may be done by persistent rubbing; and there were no towels, but the warm wind of the morning made them almost unnecessary. He got back into his clothes again with a sense of astonish-

ing well-being—except for a most persistent gnawing at his stomach.

"I wonder where we shall breakfast to-day?" he
mused as he laced his shoes. "Nowhere, most probably! Oh, well, if that dear girl can stand it, I
oughtn't to complain!"

And he fell to thinking of her, of her slim grace,
of the curve of her red lips——

"Confound it!" he said. "I can't stand it much
longer. Friendship is all very well, and the big
brother act may do for a while—but I can't keep it
up forever, and what's more, I won't!"

And then he heard her calling, in the clear, high
voice he had grown to love.

"All right!" he shouted. "Come along! '"

Presently she appeared between the trees, and he
watched her with beating heart—so straight, so sup-
ple, so perfect in every line.

"Did the magic work?" she inquired, gayly.

"Partly; but it takes more than water to remove
a two-days' growth of beard," and Stewart ran a
rueful finger over his stubbly chin. "But can it be
only two days since you burst into my room at the
Kölner Hof, and threw your arms around my neck
and kissed me!"

"Please do not speak of it!" she pleaded, with

crimson cheeks. " It was not an easy thing for a girl to do; but that spy was watching—so I nerved myself, and——"

"You did it very well, indeed," he said, reminiscently. "And to think that not once since then——"

"Once was quite enough."

"Oh, I don't blame you; I know I'm not an attractive object. People will be taking us for beauty and the beast."

"Neither the one nor the other!" she corrected.

"Well, I take back the beast; but not the beauty! You are the loveliest thing I ever saw," he added, huskily. "The very loveliest!"

She looked down at him for an instant, and her eyes were very tender; then she looked hastily away.

"There were to be no compliments until we were out of Germany," she reminded him.

"We are out of Germany," he said, and got slowly to his feet, his eyes on fire.

"No, no," she protested, backing hastily away from him. "This is German ground—let me show you!" and she ran before him out into the meadow. "Look down yonder!"

Looking down, Stewart saw the mighty army which had been mustered to crush France.

As far as the eye could reach, and from side to side of the broad valley, it stretched—masses of men and horses and wagons and artillery—masses and masses—thousands upon thousands—mile upon mile. A broad highway ran along either side of the river, and along each road a compact host moved steadily westward toward Liège.

Suddenly from the west came the thunder of heavy guns, and Stewart knew that the attack had commenced again. Again men were being driven forward to death, as they would be driven day after day, until the end, whatever that might be. And whatever it was, not a single dead man could be brought to life; not a single maimed man made whole; not a single dollar of the treasure which was being poured out like a flood could be recovered. It was all lost, wasted, worse than wasted, since it was being used to destroy, not to create! Incredible— impossible—it could not be! Even with that mighty army beneath his eyes, Stewart told himself for the hundredth time that it could not be!

The voice of his comrade broke in upon his thoughts.

" We must work our way westward along the hills until we come to the Meuse," she said. " This is the valley of the Vesdre, which flows into the Meuse, so we have only to follow it."

"Can't you prevail upon your fairy godmother to provide breakfast first?" asked Stewart. "I'm sure you have only to wish for it, and the table would appear laden with an iced melon, bacon and eggs, crisp rolls, yellow butter, and a pot of coffee—I think I can smell the coffee!" He closed his eyes and sniffed. "How perfect it would be to sit right here and eat that breakfast and watch the Germans! Oh, well," he added, as she turned away, "if not here, then somewhere else. Wait! Isn't that a house over yonder?"

It was indeed a tiny house whose gable just showed among the trees, and they made their way cautiously toward it. It stood at the side of a small garden, with two or three outbuildings about it, and it was shielded on one side by an orchard. No smoke rose from the chimney, nor was there any sign of life.

And then Stewart, who had been crouching behind the hedge beside his companion, looking at all this, rose suddenly to his feet and started forward.

"Come on," he cried; "the Germans haven't been this way—there's a chicken," and he pointed to where a plump hen was scratching industriously under the hedge.

"Here is another sign," said the girl, as they crossed the garden, and pointed to the ground. "The potatoes and turnips have not been dug."

"It must be here we're going to have that breakfast!" cried Stewart, and knocked triumphantly at the door.

There was no response and he knocked again. Then he tried the door, but it was locked. There was another door at the rear of the house, but it also was locked. There were also three windows, but they were all tightly closed with wooden shutters.

"We've got to have something to eat, that's certain," said Stewart, doggedly. "We shall have to break in," and he looked about for a weapon with which to attack the door.

"No, no," protested the girl, quickly. "That would be too like the Uhlans! Let us see if there is not some other way!"

"What other way can there be?"

"Perhaps there is none," she answered; "and if there is not, we will go on our way, and leave this house undamaged. You too seem to have been poisoned by this virus of war!"

"I only know I'm starving!" said Stewart. "If I've been poisoned by anything, it's by the virus of appetite!"

"If you were in your own country, and found yourself hungry, would you break into the first house you came to in order to get food?" she demanded. "Certainly not—you would do without food before you would do that. Is it not so?"

"Yes," said Stewart, in a low tone. "That is so. You are right."

"Perhaps I can find something," she said, more gently. "At least I will try. Remain here for a moment," and she hurried away toward the outbuildings.

Stewart stared out into the road and reflected how easy—how inevitable almost—it was to become a robber among thieves, a murderer among cutthroats. And he understood how it happens that in war even the kindliest man may become bloodthirsty, even the most honest a looter of defenseless homes.

"See what I have found!" cried a voice, and he turned to see the girl running toward him with hands outstretched. In each hand she held three eggs.

"Very well for a beginning," he commented.

" Now for the melon, the bacon, the rolls, the butter, and the coffee! "

" I fear that those must wait," she said. " Here is your breakfast," and she handed him three of the eggs.

Stewart looked at them rather blankly.

" Thanks! " he said. " But I don't quite see——"

" Then watch! "

Sitting down on the doorstep, she cracked one of her eggs gently, picked away the loosened bit of shell at its end, and put the egg to her lips.

" Oh! " he said. " So *that's* it! " and sitting down beside her, he followed her example.

He had heard of sucking eggs, but he had never before tried it, and he found it rather difficult and not particularly pleasant. But the first egg undoubtedly did assuage the pangs of hunger; the second assuaged them still more, and the third quite extinguished them. In fact, he felt a little surfeited.

" Now," she said, " for the dessert."

" Dessert! " protested Stewart. " Is there dessert? Why didn't you tell me? I never heard of dessert for breakfast, and I'm afraid I haven't room for it! "

" It will keep! " she assured him, and leading him around the larger of the outbuildings, she showed him a tree hanging thick with ruddy apples. " There are our supplies for the campaign! " she announced.

" My compliments! " he said. " You would make a great general."

They ate one or two apples and then filled their pockets. From one of hers, the girl drew a pipe and pouch of tobacco.

" Would you not like to smoke? " she asked. " I have been told that a pipe is a great comfort in times of stress! "

And Stewart, calling down blessings upon her head, filled up. Never had tobacco tasted so good, never had that old pipe seemed so sweet, as when he blew out the first puff upon the morning air.

" Salvation Yeo was right," he said. " As a hungry man's food, a sad man's cordial, a chilly man's fire, there's nothing like it under the canopy of heaven! I only wish you could enjoy it too! "

" I can enjoy your enjoyment! " she laughed as they set happily off together.

At the corner of the wood, Stewart turned for a last look at the house.

" How glad I am I didn't break in! " he said.

CHAPTER XII

AN ARMY IN ACTION

The sound of cannonading grew fiercer and fiercer, as they advanced, and the undertone of rifle fire more perceptible. It was evident that the Germans were rapidly getting more and more guns into action, and that the infantry attack was also being hotly pressed. Below them in the valley, they caught glimpses from time to time, as the trees opened out a little, of the gray-clad host marching steadily forward, as though to overwhelm the forts by sheer weight of numbers; and then, as they came out above a rocky bluff, they saw a new sight—an earnest that the Belgians were fighting to some purpose.

In a level field beside the road a long tent had been pitched, and above it floated the flag of the Red Cross. Toward it, along the road, came slowly a seemingly endless line of motor ambulances. Each of them in turn stopped opposite the tent, and white-clad assistants lifted out the stretchers, each with its huddled occupant, and carried them quickly, yet very carefully, inside the tent. In a moment the bearers were back again, pushed the empty stretchers into place, and the ambulance turned and sped swiftly back toward the battlefield. Here, too, it was evident that there was admirable and smoothly-working system—a system which alleviated, so far as it was possible to do so, the horror and the suffering of battle.

Stewart could close his eyes and see what was going on inside that tent. He could see the stripping away of the clothing, the hasty examination, the sterilization of the wound, and then, if an operation was necessary, the quick preparation, the application of the ether-cone and the swift, unerring flash of the surgeon's knife.

" That's where I should be," he said, half to himself, " I might be of some use there!" And then he turned his eyes eastward along the road. " Great heavens! Look at that gun."

Along the road below them came a monstrous cannon, mounted on a low, broad-wheeled truck, and drawn by a mighty tractor. It was of a girth so huge, of a weight evidently so tremendous, that it seemed impossible it could be handled at all, and yet it rolled along as smoothly as though it were the

merest toy. Above it stretched the heavy crane
which would swing it into the air and place it gently
on the trunnions of its carriage. Drawn by another tractor, the carriage itself came close behind—
more huge, more impressive if possible, than the gun
itself. Its tremendous wheels were encircled with
heavy blocks of steel, linked together and undulating
along the road for all the world like a monster cater-
pillar; its massive trail seemed forged to withstand
the shock of an earthquake.

" So that is the surprise! " murmured the girl beneath her breath.

And she was right. This was the surprise which
had been kept so carefully concealed—the Krupp
contribution to the war—the largest field howitzer
ever built, hurling a missile so powerful that neither
steel nor stone nor armored concrete could stand
against it.

In awed silence, the two fugitives watched this
mighty engine of destruction pass along the road to
its appointed task. Behind it came a motor truck
carrying its crew, and then a long train of ammuni-
tion carts filled with what looked like wicker baskets—but within each of those baskets lay a shell
weighing a thousand pounds! And as it passed, the
troops, opening to right and left, cheered it wildly,

for to them it meant more than victory—it meant that they would, perhaps, be spared the desperate charge with its almost certain death.

Scarcely had the first gone by, when a second gun came rolling along the road, followed by its crew and its ammunition-train; and then a third appeared, seemingly more formidable than either of the others.

"These Germans are certainly a wonderful people," said Stewart, following the three monsters with his eyes as they dwindled away westward along the road. "They may be vain and arrogant and self-confident; apparently they haven't much regard for the rights of others. But they are thorough. We must give them credit for that! They are prepared for everything."

"Yes," agreed his companion; "for everything except one thing."

"And that?"

"The spirit of a people who love liberty. Neither cannon nor armies can conquer that! The German Staff believed that Belgium would stand aside in fear."

"Surely you don't expect Belgium to win?"

"Oh, no! But every day she holds the German army here is a battle won for France. Oh, France will honor Belgium now! See—the army has been stopped. It is no longer advancing!"

What was happening to the westward they could not see, or even guess, but it was true that the helmeted host had ceased its march, had broken ranks, and was stacking arms and throwing off its accouterments in the fields along the road. The halt was to be for some time, it seemed, for everywhere camp-kitchens were being hauled into place, fires started, food unloaded.

"Come on! come on!" urged the girl. "We must reach the Meuse before this tide rolls across it."

They pressed forward again along the wooded hillside. Twice they had to cross deep valleys which ran back into the mountain, and once they had a narrow escape from a cavalry patrol which came cantering past so close upon their heels that they had barely time to throw themselves into the underbrush. They could see, too, that even in the hills caution was necessary, for raiding parties had evidently struck up into them, as was proved by an occasional column of smoke rising from a burning house. Once they came upon an old peasant with a face wrinkled like a withered apple, sitting staring down at the German host, so preoccupied that he did not even raise his eyes as they passed. And at last they came out above the broad plain where the Vesdre flows into the Meuse.

Liège, with its towers and terraced streets, was concealed from them by a bend in the river and by a bold bluff which thrust out toward it from the east —a bluff crowned by a turreted fortress—perhaps the same they had seen the night before—which was vomiting flame and iron down into the valley.

The trees and bushes which clothed its sides concealed the infantry which was doubtless lying there, but in the valley just below them they could see a battery of heavy guns thundering against the Belgian fort. So rapidly were they served that the roar of their discharge was almost continuous, while high above it rose the scream of the shells as they hurtled toward their mark. There was something fascinating in the precise, calculated movement of the gunners—one crouching on the trail, one seated on either side of the breech, four others passing up the shells from the caisson close at hand. Their officer was watching the effect of the fire through a field-glass, and speaking a word of direction now and then.

Their fire was evidently taking effect, for it was this battery which the gunners in the fort were trying to silence—trying blindly, for the German guns were masked by a high hedge and a strip of orchard, and only a tenuous, quickly-vanishing wisp of white smoke marked the discharge. So the Belgian gunners dropped their shells hither and yon, hoping that chance might send one of them home.

They did not find the battery, but they found other marks—a beautiful white villa, on the first slope of the hillside, was torn asunder like a house of cards and a moment later was in flames; a squad of cavalry, riding gayly back from a reconnoissance down the river, was violently scattered; a peasant family, father and mother and three children, hastening along the road to a place of safety, was instantly blotted out.

It was evident now that the Meuse was the barrier which had stopped the army. Far up toward Liège were the ruins of a bridge, and no doubt all the others had been blown up by the Belgians.

Down by the river-bank a large force of engineers were working like mad to throw a pontoon across the swift current. The material had already been brought up—heavy, flat-bottomed boats, carried on wagons drawn by motor-tractors, great beams and planks, boxes of bolts—everything, in a word, needed to build this bridge just here at a point which had no doubt been selected long in advance! The bridge shot out into the river with a speed which seemed to Stewart almost miraculous. Boat after boat was towed into place and anchored firmly; great beams were bolted into position, each of them fitting exactly; and then the heavy planks were laid with the precision and rapidity of a machine. Indeed, Stewart told himself, it was really a machine that he was watching—a machine of flesh and blood, wonderfully trained for just such feats as this.

"Look! look!" cried the girl, and Stewart, following her pointing finger, saw an aëroplane sweeping toward them from the direction of the city. Evidently the defenders of the fort, weary of firing blindly at a battery they could not see, were sending a scout to uncover it.

The aëroplane flew very high at first—so high that the two men in it appeared the merest specks, but almost at once two high-angle guns were banging away at it, though the shells fell far short. Gradually it circled lower and lower, as if quite unconscious of the marksmen in the valley, and as it swept past the hill, Stewart glimpsed the men quite plainly —one with his hands upon the levers, the other, with a pair of glasses to his eyes, eagerly scanning the ground beneath.

And then Stewart, happening to glance toward the

horizon, was held enthralled by a new spectacle. High over the hills to the east flew a mammoth shape, straight toward the fort. Its defenders saw their danger instantly, and hastily elevating some of their guns, greeted the Zeppelin with a salvo. But it came straight on with incredible speed, and as it passed above the fort, a terrific explosion shook the mountain to its base. Stewart, staring with bated breath, told himself that that was the end, that not one stone of that great fortress remained upon another; but an instant later, another volley sent after the fleeing airship told that the fort still stood—that the bomb had missed its mark.

The aëroplane scouts, their vision shadowed by the broad wings of their machine, had not seen the Zeppelin until the explosion brought them sharp round toward it. Then, with a sudden upward swoop, they leaped forward in pursuit. But nothing could overtake that monster,—it was speeding too fast, it was already far away, and in a moment disappeared over the hills to the west. So, after a moment's breathless flight, the biplane turned, circled slowly above the fort, and dropped down toward the town behind it.

Five minutes later, a high-powered shell burst squarely in the midst of the German battery, disabling two of the guns. At once the horses were driven up and the remaining guns whirled away to a new emplacement, while a passing motor ambulance was stopped to pick up the wounded.

Stewart, who had been watching all this with something of the feelings of a spectator at some tremendous panorama, was suddenly conscious of a mighty stream of men approaching the river from the head of the valley. A regiment of cavalry rode in front, their long lances giving them an appearance indescribably picturesque; behind them came column after column of infantry, moving like clock-work, their gray uniforms blending so perfectly with the background that it was difficult to tell where the columns began or where they ended. Their passage reminded Stewart of the quiver of heat above a sultry landscape—a vibration of the air scarcely perceptible.

All the columns were converging on the river, and looking toward it, Stewart saw that the bridge was almost done. As the last planks were laid, a squadron of Uhlans, which had been held in readiness, dashed across, and deploying fanshape, advanced to reconnoiter the country on the other side.

"That looks like invasion in earnest!" said Stewart.

The girl nodded without replying, her eyes on the advancing columns. The cavalry was the first to reach the bridge, and filed rapidly across to reënforce their comrades; then the infantry pressed forward in solid column. Stewart could see how the boats settled deep in the water under the tremendous weight.

High above all other sounds, came the hideous shriek of a great shell, which flew over the bridge and exploded in the water a hundred yards below it. A minute later, there came another shriek, but this time the shell fell slightly short. But the third shell —the third shell!

Surely, Stewart told himself, the bridge will be cleared; that close-packed column will not be exposed to a risk so awful. But it pressed on, without a pause, without a break. What must be the soldiers' thoughts, as they waited for the third shell!

Again that high, hideous, blood-curdling shriek split through the air, and the next instant a shell exploded squarely in the middle of the bridge. Stewart had a moment's vision of a tangle of shattered bodies, then he saw that the bridge was gone and the river filled with drowning men, weighed down by their heavy accouterments. He could hear

their shrill cries of terror as they struggled in the
current; then the cries ceased as the river swept most
of them away. Only a very few managed to reach
the bank.

Stewart hid his face in his trembling hands. It
was too hideous! It could not be! He could not
bear it—the world would not bear it, if it knew!

A sharp cry from his companion told him that the
awful drama was not yet played to an end. She was
pointing beyond the river, where the cavalry and the
small body of infantry which had got across seemed
thrown into sudden confusion. Horses reared and
fell, men dropped from their saddles. The infantry threw themselves forward upon their faces;
and then to Stewart's ears came the sharp rattle of
musketry.

" The Belgians are attacking them! " cried the
girl. " They are driving them back! "

But that cavalry, so superbly trained, that infantry, so expertly officered, were not to be driven back
without a struggle. The Uhlans formed into line
and swept forward, with lances couched, over the
ridge beyond the river and out of sight, in a furious
charge. But the Belgians must have stood firm, for
at the end of a few moments, the troopers straggled
back again, sadly diminished in numbers, and rode

rapidly away down the river, leaving the infantry to its fate.

Meanwhile, on the eastern bank of the river, a battery of quick-firers had already been swung into position, and was singing its deadly tune to hold the Belgians back. Already the men of that little company on the farther side had found a sort of refuge behind a line of hummocks. Already some heavier guns were being hurried into position to defend the bridge which the engineers began at once to rebuild farther down the stream, where it would be better masked from the fort's attack.

Evidently the Belgians did not intend to enter that deadly zone of fire, and the fight settled down to a dogged, long-distance one.

" We cannot get across here," said the girl at last. " We shall have to work our way downstream until we are past the Germans. If we can join the Belgians, we are safe."

But to get past the Germans proved a far greater task than they had anticipated. There seemed to be no end to the gray-clad legions. Brigade after brigade packed the stretch of level ground along the river, while the road was crowded with an astounding tangle of transport wagons, cook wagons, armored motors, artillery, tractors, ambulances, and automobiles of every sort, evidently seized by the army in its advance.

As he looked at them, Stewart could not but wonder how on earth they had ever been assembled here, and, still more, how they were ever going to be got away again.   Also, he thought, how easily might they be cut to pieces by a few batteries of machine-guns posted on that ridge across the river! Looking across, he saw that the army chiefs had foreseen that danger and guarded against it, for a strong body of cavalry had been thrown across the river to screen the advance, while along the bank, behind hasty but well-built intrenchments, long lines of artillery had been massed to repel any attack from that direction.

But no attack came. The little Belgian army evidently had its hands full elsewhere, and was very busy indeed, as the roar of firing both up and down the river testified. And then, as the fugitives walked on along the hillside, they saw that one avenue of advance would soon be open, for a company of engineers, heavily guarded by cavalry and quick-firers, was repairing a bridge whose central span had been blown up by the Belgians as they retreated.

The bridge had connected two little villages, that on the east bank dominated by a beautiful white château placed at the edge of a cliff. Of the villages little remained but smoking ruins, and a flag above the château showed that it had been converted into a staff headquarters.

Where was the owner of the château, Stewart wondered, looking up at it. Where were the women who had sat and gossiped on its terrace? Where were all the people who had lived in those two villages? Wandering somewhere to the westward, homeless and destitute, every one of them—haggard women and hungry children and tottering old men, whose quiet world had turned suddenly to chaos.

" Well," he said, at last, " it looks as if we shall have to wait until these fellows clear out. We can't get across the river as long as there is a line like that before it."

" Perhaps when they begin to advance, they will leave a break in the line somewhere," his companion suggested. " Or perhaps we can slip across in the darkness. Let us wait and see."

So they sat down behind the screen of a clump of bushes, and munched their apples, while they watched the scene below. Stewart even ventured to light his pipe again.

A flotilla of boats of every shape and size, commandeered, no doubt, all up and down the river, plied busily back and forth, augmenting the troops

on the other side as rapidly as possible; and again
Stewart marveled at the absolute order and system
preserved in this operation, which might so easily
have become confused. There was no crowding, no
overloading, no hurrying, but everywhere a calm
and efficient celerity. A certain number of men
entered each of the boats,—leading their horses by
the bridle, if they were cavalry,—and the boats
pushed off. Reluctant horses were touched with a
whip, but most of them stepped down into the water
quietly and without hesitation, showing that they
had been drilled no less than their masters, and
swam strongly along beside the boat. On the other
shore, the disembarkation was conducted in the same
unhurried fashion, and the boat swung back into the
stream again for another load.

But a great army cannot be conveyed across a
river in small boats, and it was not until mid-after-
noon, when the repairs on the bridge were finished,
that the real forward movement began. From that
moment it swept forward like a flood—first the remainder of the cavalry, then the long batteries of
quick-firers, then regiment after regiment of infantry, each regiment accompanied by its transport.
Looking down at the tangle of wagons and guns
and motors, Stewart saw that it was not really a

tangle, but an ordered arrangement, which unrolled itself smoothly and without friction.

The advance was slow, but it was unceasing, and by nightfall at least fifteen thousand men had crossed the river. Still the host encamped along it seemed as great as ever. As one detachment crossed, another came up from somewhere in the rear to take its place. Stewart's brain reeled as he gazed down at them and tried to estimate their number; and this was only one small corner of the Kaiser's army. For leagues and leagues to north and south it was pressing forward; no doubt along the whole frontier similar hosts were massed for the invasion. It was gigantic, incredible—that word was in his thoughts more frequently than any other. He could not believe his own eyes; his brain refused to credit the evidence of his senses.

Each unit of this great array, each company, each squad, seemed to live its own life and to be sufficient unto itself. Stewart could see the company cooks preparing the evening meal; the heavy, wheeled camp-stoves were fired up, great kettles of soup were set bubbling, broad loaves of dark bread were cut into thick slices; and finally, at a bugle call, the men fell into line, white-enameled cups in hand, and received their rations. It seemed to Stewart that he could smell the appetizing odor of that thick soup—an odor of onions and potatoes and turnips.

"Doesn't it make you ravenous?" he asked. "Wouldn't you like to have some real solid food to set your teeth into? Raw eggs and apples—ugh!"

"Yes, it does," said the girl, who had been contemplating the scene with dreamy eyes, scarcely speaking all the afternoon. "The French still wear the uniform of 1870," she added, half to herself; "a long bulky blue coat and red trousers."

"Visible a mile away—while these fellows melt into the ground at a hundred yards! If Germany wins, it will be through forethought!"

"But she cannot win!" protested the girl, fiercely. "She must not win!"

"Well, all I can say is that France has a big job ahead!"

"France will not stand alone! Already she has Russia as an ally; Belgium is doing what it can; Servia has a well-tried army. Nor are those all! England will soon find that she cannot afford to stand aside, and if there is need, other nations will come in—Portugal, Rumania, even Italy!"

Stewart shook his head, skeptically.

"I don't know," he said, slowly. "I know noth-

ing about world-politics, but I don't believe any nation will come in that doesn't have to!"

" That is it—all of them will find that they have
to, for Prussian triumph means slavery for all Europe—for the Germans most of all. It is for them
as much as for herself that France is fighting—for
human rights everywhere—for the poor people who
till the fields, and toil in the factories, and sweat in
the mines! And civilization must fight with her
against this barbarian state ruled by the upturned
mustache and mailed fist, believing that might makes
right and that she can do no wrong! That is why
you and I are fighting on France's side!"

" If nobody fights any harder than I——"

She stopped him with a hand upon his arm.

" Ah, but you are fighting well! One can fight
in other ways than with a rifle—one can fight with
one's brains."

" It is your brains, not mine, which have done the
fighting in this campaign," Stewart pointed out.

" Where should I have been but for you? Dead,
most probably, my message lost, my life-work shattered!"

He placed his hand quietly over hers and held it
fast.

" Let us be clear, then," he said. " It is not for

freedom, or for any abstract ideal I am fighting. It is for you—for your friendship, for your——"

" No, it is for France," she broke in. " I am not worth fighting for—I am but one girl among many millions. And if we win—if we get through——"

She paused, gazing out through the gathering darkness with starry eyes.

" Yes—if we get through," he prompted.

" It will mean more to France than many regiments ! " and she struck the pocket which contained the letters. " Ah, we must get through—we must not fail ! "

She rose suddenly and stretched her arms high above her head.

" Dear God, you will not let us fail ! " she cried. Then she turned and held out a hand to him. " Come," she said, quietly ; " if we are to get across, it must be before the moon rises."

CHAPTER XIII

THE PASSAGE OF THE MEUSE

THE mist of early evening had settled over the river and wiped away every vestige of the army, save the flaring lights of the camp-kitchens and the white lamps of the motors; but the creaking of wheels, the pounding of engines, and the regular tramp of countless feet told that the advance had not slackened for an instant.

On the uplands there was still a little light, and Stewart and his companion picked their way cautiously down through a belt of woodland, across a rough field, and over a wall, beyond which they found an uneven path, made evidently by a vanished herd as it went back and forth to its pasture. They advanced slowly and silently, every sense on the alert, but seemingly no pickets had been posted on this side, from which there was no reason to fear an attack, and they were soon down amid the mist, at the edge of the encampment.

Here, however, there were sentries—a close line of them; the fugitives could see them dimly outlined against the fires, and could hear their occasional interchange of challenges.

"It is impossible to get through here," whispered the girl. "Let us go on until we are below the bridge. Perhaps we shall find a gap there."

So, hand in hand lest they become separated in the darkness, they worked their way cautiously downstream, just out of sight of the line of sentries.

"Wait!" whispered Stewart, suddenly. "What is that ahead?"

Something tall and black and vaguely menacing loomed above them into the night.

"The church tower!" breathed the girl, after a moment. "See—there are ruins all about it—it is the village they burned."

They hesitated. Should they enter it, or try to go around? There was something sinister and threatening about these roofless, blackened walls which had once been homes; but to go around meant climbing cliffs, meant breathless scrambling—above all, meant loss of time.

"We must risk it," said the girl, at last. "We can come back if the place is guarded."

Their hands instinctively tightened their clasp as they stole forward into the shadow of the houses, along what had once been a street, but was now littered and blocked with fallen walls and débris of every kind, some of it still smouldering. Everywhere there was the stench of half-burned wood, and another stench, more penetrating, more nauseating.

Stewart was staring uneasily about him, telling himself that that stench could not possibly be what it seemed, when his companion's hand squeezed his and dragged him quickly aside against a wall.

" Down, down ! " she breathed, and they cowered together behind a mass of fallen masonry.

Then Stewart peered out, cautiously. Yes, there was someone coming. Far down the street ahead of them a tiny light flashed, disappeared, flashed again, and disappeared.

Crowding close together, they buried themselves deeper in the ruins and waited.

At last they could hear steps—slow, cautious steps, full of fear—and the light appeared again, dancing from side to side. It seemed to be a small lantern, carefully shaded, so that only a narrow beam of light escaped; and that beam was sent dancing from side to side along the street, in dark corners, under fallen doorways.

Suddenly it stopped, and Stewart's heart leaped sickeningly as he saw that the beam rested on a face —a white face, staring up with sightless eyes.

The light approached, hung above it—a living hand caught up the dead one, on which there was the gleam of gold, a knife flashed——

And then, from the darkness almost beside them, four darts of flame stabbed toward the kneeling figure, and the ruins rocked with a great explosion.

When Stewart opened his eyes again, he saw a squad of soldiers, each armed with an electric torch, standing about the body of the robber of the dead, while their sergeant emptied his pockets. There were rings—one still encircling a severed finger—money, a watch, trinkets of every sort, some of them quite worthless.

The man was in uniform, and the sergeant, ripping open coat and shirt, drew out the little identifying tag of metal which hung about his neck, broke it from its string, and thrust it into his pocket. Then he gathered the booty into his handkerchief, tied the ends together with a satisfied grunt, and gave a gruff command. The lights vanished and the squad stumbled ahead into the darkness.

There was a moment's silence. Stewart's nerves were quivering so that he could scarcely control them —he could feel his mouth twitching, and put his hand up to stop it.

" We can't go on," he muttered. " We must go back. This is too horrible—it is unbearable! "

Together they stole tremblingly out of the ruin, along the littered street, past the church-tower, across the road, over the wall, back into the clean fields. There they flung themselves down gaspingly, side by side.

How sweet the smell of the warm earth, after the stench of the looted town! How calm and lovely the stars.

Stewart, staring up at them, felt a great serenity descend upon him. After all, what did it matter to the universe—this trivial disturbance upon this tiny planet? Men might kill each other, nations disappear; but the stars would swing on in their courses, the constellations go their predestined ways. Of what significance was man in the great scheme of things? How absurd the pomp of kings and kaisers, how grotesque their assumption of greatness!

A stifled sob startled him. He groped quickly for his comrade, and found her lying prone, her face buried in her arms. He drew her close and held her as he might have held a child. After all, she was scarcely more than that—a child, delicate and sensitive. As a child might, she pillowed her head upon his breast and lay there sobbing softly.

But the sobs ceased presently; he could feel how she struggled for self-control; and at last she turned in his arms and lay staring up at the heavens.

"That's right," he said. "Look up at the stars! That helps!" and it seemed to him, in spite of the tramp of feet and the rattle of wheels and curses of savage drivers, that they were alone together in the midst of things, and that nothing else mattered.

"How sublime they are!" she whispered. "How they calm and strengthen one! They seem to understand!" She turned her face and looked at him. "You too have understood!" she said, very softly; then gently disengaged his arms and sat erect.

"Do you know," said Stewart, slowly, "what we saw back there has revived my faith in human nature—and it needed reviving! Those men must have seen that that scoundrel was a soldier like themselves, yet they didn't hesitate to shoot. Justice still lives, then; a sense of decency can survive, even in an army. I had begun to doubt it, and I am glad to know that I was wrong."

"The tenderest, noblest gentleman I ever knew," she answered, softly, "was a soldier."

"Yes," Stewart agreed; "I have known one or two like that."

War was not wholly bad, then. Its fierce flame blasted, blackened, tortured—but it also refined. It had its brutal lusts—but it had also its high heroisms!

The girl at his side stirred suddenly.

" We must be going," she said.

" You're sure you are all right again? "

" Yes," and she rose quickly. " We must go back the way we came."

They set out again along the edge of the army, stumbling across rough fields, crouching behind hedges, turning aside to avoid a lighted house where some officers were making merry. For perhaps a mile they pressed on, with a line of sentries always at their right, outlined against the gleam of scattered lights. Then, quite suddenly, there were no more lights, and they knew that they had reached the limit of the encampment.

Had they also reached the limit of the line of sentries? There was no way to make sure; but they crept forward to the wall along the highway and peered cautiously over. The road seemed empty. They crossed it as swiftly and silently as shadows, and in a moment were safe behind the wall on the other side.

Beyond it lay the yard of an iron foundry, with

great piles of castings scattered about and a tall
building looming at their left. In front of it they
caught the gleam of a sentry's rifle, so they bore
away to the right until they reached the line of the
railway running close along the river bank. There
were sentries here, too, but they were stationed far
apart and were apparently half-asleep, and the fugitives had no difficulty in slipping between them. A
moment later, they had scrambled down a steep bank
and stood at the edge of the river.

"And now," whispered Stewart, "to get over."

He looked out across the water, flowing strong
and deep, mysterious and impressive in the darkness,
powerful, unhurried, alert—as if grimly conscious
of its task, and rejoicing in it; for this stream which
was holding the Germans back had its origin away
southward in the heart of France. He could not see
the other bank, but he knew that it was at least two
hundred yards away.

"If we could find a boat!" he added. "We saw
plenty of them this afternoon."

"We dare not use a boat," the girl objected.
"We should be seen and fired upon."

"Do you mean to swim?" Stewart demanded.

"Be more careful!" she cautioned. "Someone
may hear us," and she drew him down into the

shadow of the bank. " Unfortunately, I cannot swim, but no doubt you can."

"I'm not what would be called an expert, but I think I could swim across this river. However, I absolutely refuse to try to take you over. It would be too great a risk."

"If we had a plank or log, I could hold to it while you pushed it along. If you grew tired, you could rest and drift for a time."

Stewart considered the plan. It seemed feasible. A drifting plank would attract no attention from the shore—the river was full of débris from the operations around Liège—and, whether they got across or not, there would be no danger of either of them drowning. And they ought to get over, for it would be no great task to work a plank across the stream.

"Yes, I think I could do that," he said at last. "Let us see if we can find a plank."

There was nothing of the sort along the shore, though they searched it for some distance; but opposite the foundry they came upon a pile of the square wooden sand-boxes in which castings are made. Stewart, when he saw them, chuckled with satisfaction.

"Just the thing!" he said. " Providence is certainly on our side to-night!"

"I hope so!" breathed the girl, and between them they carried one of the boxes down to the edge of the water.

Then, after a moment's hesitation, Stewart sat down and began to take off his shoes.

"We shall have to get rid of our clothing," he said, in the most matter-of-fact tone he could muster. "There is nothing heavier than clothes when they get water-soaked. Besides, we've got to keep them dry if we can. If we don't, we shall nearly freeze to death after we leave the water—and they'll betray us a mile off!"

The girl stood for a moment staring out across the river. Then she sat down with her back to him.

"You are quite right," she agreed, quietly, and bent above her shoes.

"We'll turn the box upside down and put our clothes upon it," went on Stewart, cheerfully. "They will keep dry there. The water isn't very cold, probably, but we shall be mighty glad to have some dry things to get into once we are out of it."

She did not reply, and Stewart went rapidly on with his undressing. When that was finished, he rolled his trousers, shoes and underclothing into a compact bundle inside his coat, and tied the sleeves together.

"Now I'm going to launch the raft," he said. "Roll your clothes up inside your coat, so that nothing white will show, and wade out to me as soon as you are ready."

"Very well," she answered, in a low tone.

With his bundle under one arm, Stewart turned the box over and dragged it into the water. He had been shivering in the night air, but the water was agreeably warm. Placing his bundle upon the top of the box, he pushed it before him out into the stream, and was soon breast-deep. Then, holding the box against the current, he waited.

Minute after minute passed, but she did not come. He could not see the shore, but he strained his eyes toward it, wondering if he should go back, if anything had happened. So quiet and unquestioning had been her acceptance of his plan that he did not suspect the struggle waging there on the bank between girlish modesty and grim necessity.

But, at last, from the mist along the shore, a white figure emerged, dim and ghostlike in the darkness, and he heard a gentle splashing as she came toward him through the water. He raised his arm, to make certain that she saw him, then turned his head away.

Near and nearer came the splashing; then the box rocked gently as she placed her clothing on it.

" All right? " he asked, softly.

" Yes," she answered.

He turned to find her looking up at him from the level of the stream, which came just beneath her chin. The light of the stars reflected on the water crowned her with a misty halo, and again he read in her face that sweet and tremulous appeal for respect and understanding which had so moved him once before. It moved him far more deeply now; but he managed to bite back the words which leaped to his lips and to speak almost casually—as though situations such as this were the most ordinary in the world.

" Have you got a firm grip of the handle? "

" Yes."

He assured himself that both bundles of clothing were secure.

" All ready, then," he said. " Just hold on and let your body float out in the water. Don't hold your head too high, and if you feel your hands slipping call me at once. I don't want to lose you, little comrade ! "

" I will remember," she promised, smiling gratefully up at him.

" Then here we go," and he pushed the box slowly out into the stream.

In a moment the water was at his chin.

" All right? " he asked again.

" Yes."

He took another step forward, the current caught him and lifted him off his feet, and he began to swim easily and slowly. He was not sure of his strength, it was a long time since he had done any serious swimming, and he knew that he must husband himself. Then, too, the current was stronger than it had seemed from the shore, and he found that he could make head against it but slowly, for the box was of an awkward shape and the girl's body trailing behind it so much dead weight.

" Slow but sure," he said, reassuringly, resting a moment. " You're quite all right? "

" Yes. You must not worry about me."

He glanced back at the shore, where the lights of the camp shone dimly through the mist.

" We're going to drift right past the camp," he said; " but they can't see us, and it will make our landing safer if we come out below the troops. It would be rather embarrassing, wouldn't it, if we found a patrol waiting for us on the bank? Now for another swim! "

He pushed ahead until he found himself beginning to tire, then stopped and looked around.

" There's the bridge! " he said, suddenly.

And, sure enough, just ahead, they could see its dim shape spanning the stream. A cold fear gripped Stewart's heart. Suppose they should be swept against one of the abutments!

"Take tight hold with both hands," he commanded. "Don't let go, whatever happens!"

He swung himself round to the front of the box and tried to pierce the gloom ahead. The center of the stream would be clear, he told himself, and they must be nearly in the center. Then he heard the confused tread of many feet, the current seemed to quicken, and he glanced up to see that they were almost beneath the bridge. Yes, the stream ahead was clear; but what were those lights down along the water?

And then he saw that a boat was moored there, and that a squad of men were strengthening the supports with which the engineers had hastily repaired the shattered abutment.

With frenzied energy, he pulled the box around so that his companion's head was hidden behind it; then, with only his nose out, he floated silently on. They would not see him, he told himself; they were too busily at work. Even if they did, they could make nothing of this rough shape drifting down the river.

Nevertheless, as they swept within the circle of light cast by the flaring torches, Stewart, taking a deep breath, let himself sink below the surface; and not until the blood was singing in his ears did he come up again.

They had passed! They were safe! He drew a deep breath. Then he peered around the box.

"Are you there? Are you all right?"

"Yes," came the soft answer. "Never tell me again that you are not a fighter!"

"Compliments are barred until we are safe in Belgium!" he reminded her gayly. "But it's clear sailing now!"

He struck out again, pushing diagonally forward toward the bank which he could not see, but which could not be far away. This was not going to prove such a desperate adventure, after all. The worst was over, for, once on land, far below the German troops, they had only to push forward to find themselves among friends.

Then his heart stood still as a shrill scream rent the night—a woman's scream of deadly horror—and he jerked his head around to find that his comrade was no longer there.

CHAPTER XIV.

THE LAST DASH

NEVER will Stewart forget the stark horror of that instant; never afterward did he think of it without a shudder. It was one of those instants—fortunately few—which stamp themselves indelibly upon the brain, which penetrate the spirit, which leave a mark not to be effaced.

It was the flash of her white arm, as she sank for the second time, that saved her. Instinctively Stewart clutched at it, seized it, regained the box at a vigorous stroke, threw one arm across a handle, and raised her head above the water.

Her face was white as death, her eyes were closed, she hung a dead weight upon his arm—and yet, Stewart told himself, she could not have drowned in so short a time. She had been under water only a few seconds. Perhaps she had been wounded—but he had heard no shot. His teeth chattered as he looked at her, she lay so still, so deathlike.

And then he remembered that shrill scream of ut-

ter horror. Why had she screamed? What was
it had wrung from her that terrible cry? Had some
awful thing touched her, seized her, tried to drag
her down?

Shivering with fear, Stewart looked out across the
water. Was there something lurking in those depths
—some horror—some unthinkable monster——

He shook himself impatiently; he must not give
way to his nerves. Holding her face back, he
splashed some water into it, gently at first, then more
violently. She was not dead—she had only fainted.
A touch on her temple assured him that her heart
was beating.

He must have been unconsciously paddling against
the current, for something touched him gently on the
shoulder—a piece of driftwood, perhaps; and then
he was suddenly conscious that it was not driftwood
—that it was soft, hairy——

He spun around, to find himself staring down into
a pair of unseeing eyes, set in a face so puffed and
leprous as to be scarcely human.

How he repressed the yell of terror that rose in
his throat he never knew; but he *did* repress it somehow, and creeping with horror, pushed the box
quickly to one side. But the bloated body, caught in
the swirl of his wake, turned and followed, with

an appearance of malignant purpose which sent a
chill up Stewart's spine. Kicking frenziedly, he held
the box back against the current, and for an instant
fancied that his hideous pursuer was holding back
also. But, after what seemed like a moment's hesitation, it drifted on down the stream and vanished
in the darkness.

For a moment longer, Stewart stared after it,
half-expecting it to reappear and bear down upon
him. Then, with an anguished breath of relief, he
stopped swimming and looked down at the face upon
his arm. So that was the horror which had beset
her. She had felt it nuzzling against her, had turned
as he had done! No wonder she had screamed!

He felt her bosom rise and fall with a quick gasp;
then her eyes opened and gazed up at him. For an
instant they gazed vacantly and wildly, then a flood
of crimson swept from chin to brow, and she struggled to free herself from his encircling arm.

" Easy now! " Stewart protested. " Are you sure
you're all right? Are you sure you're strong enough
to hold on? "

" Yes, yes! " she panted. " Let me go! "

He guided her fingers to the handles, assured
himself that she grasped them firmly, then released
her and swam to his old position on the other side

of the box. For a moment they floated on in silence.

"How foolish of me!" she said, at last, in a choking voice. "I suppose you saved my life!"

"Oh, I just grabbed you by the arm and held on to you till you came to."

"Did I scream?"

"I should rather think so! Scared me nearly to death!"

"I could not help it! I was frightened. It was— it was——"

"I know," said Stewart, quickly. "I saw it. Don't think about it—it has gone on downstream."

"It—it seemed to be following me!" she gasped.

"Yes—I had the same feeling; but it's away ahead of us now. Now, if you're all right, we'll work in toward the bank—it can't be far off. Hullo! What's that?"

A shadowy shape emerged from the darkness along the eastern shore, and they caught the rattle of oars in row-locks.

"They heard you scream," whispered Stewart. "They've sent out a patrol to investigate," and with all his strength he pushed on toward the farther bank.

Suddenly a shaft of light shot from the bow of the boat out across the water, sweeping up and down, dwelling upon this piece of driftwood and upon that. With a gasp of apprehension, Stewart swung the box around so that it screened them from the search-light, and kept on swimming with all his strength.

"If they spot those bundles," he panted, "they'll be down upon us like a load of brick! Ah!"

The light was upon them. Above their heads the bundles of clothing stood out as if silhouetted against the midday sky. Stewart cursed his folly in placing them there; surely wet clothes were preferable to capture! He should not have taken the risk—he should have put the clothing inside the box and let it take its chance. But it was too late now. In another moment——

The light swept on.

From sheer reaction, Stewart's body dropped limply for an instant through the water, and then rebounded as from an electric shock.

"I can touch bottom!" he said, hoarsely. "We'll get there yet. Hold fast!"

Setting his teeth, digging his toes into the mud, he dragged the box toward the shore with all his strength. In a moment, the water was only to his shoulders—to his chest—he could see that his comrade was wading, too,

He stopped, peering anxiously ahead. There was

no light anywhere along the shore, and no sound broke the stillness.

"It seems all right," he whispered. "I will go ahead and make sure. If it is safe, you will hear me whistle. Keep behind the box, for fear that searchlight will sweep this way again, and when I whistle, come straight out. You understand?"

"Yes."

"Good-by, then, for a moment, little comrade!"

"Good-by."

With one look deep into her eyes, he snatched up the bundle containing his clothing, and crouching as low in the water as he could, set off cautiously toward the shore. There was a narrow strip of gravel just ahead, and behind that a belt of darkness which, he told himself, was a wood. He could see no sign of any sentry.

As he turned at the water's edge, he noticed a growing band of light over the hills to the east, and knew that the moon was rising. There was no time to lose! He whistled softly and began hastily to dress.

Low as the whistle was, it reached the boat—or perhaps it was mere chance that brought the searchlight sweeping round just as the girl rose in the water and started toward the shore. The light

swept past her, swept back again, and stopped full
upon the flying figure, as slim and graceful as
Diana's.

There was a hoarse shout from the boat, and the
splash of straining oars; and then Stewart was
dashing forward into the water, was by her side, had
caught her hand and was dragging her toward the
bank.

"Go on! Go on!" he cried, and paused to pick
up his shoes, for the sharp gravel warned him, that,
with unprotected feet, flight would be impossible.
His coat lay beside them and he grabbed that too.
Then he was up again and after her, across the
cruel stones of the shore, toward the darkness of the
wood and safety—one yard—two yards——

And always the searchlight beat upon them merci-
lessly.

There came a roar of rifles from the river, a
flash of flame, the whistle of bullets about his ears.

And then they were in the wood and he had her
by the hand.

"Not hurt?" he gasped.

"No, no!"

"Thank heaven! We are safe for a moment.
Get on some clothes—especially your shoes. We
can't run barefooted!"

He was fumbling with his own shoes as he spoke —managed to thrust his bruised feet into them— stuffed his socks into the pocket of his coat and slipped into it.

"Ready?" he asked.

"In a moment!"

And then he felt her hand in his.

"Which way?"

He glanced back through the trees. The boat was at the bank; its occupants were leaping out, rifles in hand; the searchlight swept up and down.

"This way, I think!" and he guided her diagonally to the right. "Go carefully! The less noise we make the better. But as long as those fellows keep on shooting, they can't hear us."

Away they went, stumbling, scrambling, bending low to escape the overhanging branches, saving each other from some ugly falls—up a long incline covered by an open wood, across a little glade, over a wall, through another strip of woodland, into a road, over another wall—and then Stewart gave a gasp of relief, for they were in a field of grain.

"We shall be safe here," he said, as they plunged into it. "I will watch, while you finish dressing," and he faced back toward the way they had come.

The full moon was sailing high above the eastern

hills, and he could see distinctly the wall they had just crossed, with the white road behind it, and beyond that the dense shadow of the wood. It was on the strip of road he kept his eyes, but no living creature crossed it, and at last he felt a touch upon his arm.

" My turn now ! " the girl whispered.

Stewart sat down upon the ground, wiped the mud from his feet, shook the gravel from his shoes, drew on his socks and laced his shoes properly. As he started to get up, he felt a sudden sharp twinge in his shoulder.

" What is it ? " asked the girl, quickly, for an exclamation of pain had burst from him before he could choke it back.

" Nothing at all ! " he said, and rose, gingerly. " I touched a raw place, where a briar scratched me. I seem to be composed largely of raw places—especially as to my feet. How are yours ? "

" One of them hurts a little—not enough to mention."

" You're sure you can walk ? "

" Certainly—or run, if need be."

" Then we had better push on a little farther. The Germans are still too close for comfort. Keep your back to the moon—I'll act as rear-guard."

For a moment she looked up questioningly into his face.

"You are sure you are not hurt?" she asked.

"Perfectly sure."

"I was afraid you had been shot—I saw how you placed yourself between me and the river!"

"The merest accident," he assured her. "Besides, those fellows couldn't shoot!"

She gazed up at him yet a moment, her lips quivering; then she turned and started westward through the field.

Falling in behind, Stewart explored his wounded shoulder cautiously with his fingers. He could feel that his shirt was wet with blood, but the stabbing pain had been succeeded by a sharp stinging which convinced him that it was only a flesh-wound. Folding his shirt back, he found it at last, high in the shoulder above the collar-bone.

"That was lucky!" he told himself, as he pressed his handkerchief over it, rebuttoned his shirt, and pushed on after his comrade. "Half an inch lower and the bone would have been smashed!"

Away to the south, they could hear the thunder of the Liège forts, and Stewart, aching from his own slight injury, thought with a shudder of the poor fellows who had to face that deadly fire. No doubt it was to this fresh attack the troops had been marched which they had seen crossing the river. It was improbable that the invaders would risk pushing westward until the forts were reduced; and so, when the fugitives came presently to a road which ran northwestwardly, they ventured to follow it.

"We would better hide somewhere and rest till daylight," Stewart suggested, at last. "We have had a hard day."

He himself was nearly spent with fatigue and hunger, and his shoulder was stiff and sore.

"Very well," the girl agreed. "I too am very tired. Where shall we go?"

Stewart stopped and looked about him.

On one side of the road was a level pasture affording no shelter; on the other side, a rolling field mounted to a strip of woodland.

"At the edge of those trees would be the best place," he decided, and the girl agreed with a nod.

Laboriously they clambered over the wall beside the road and set off toward this refuge. The field was very rough and seemed interminable, and more than once Stewart thought that he must drop where he stood; but they reached the wood at last and threw themselves down beneath the first clump of undergrowth.

Stewart was asleep almost before he touched the ground; but the girl lay for a long time with eyes open, staring up into the night. Then, very softly, she crawled to Stewart's side, raised herself on one elbow and looked down into his face.

It was not at all the face of the man she had met at the Kölner Hof two days before. It was thinner and paler; there were dark circles of exhaustion under the eyes; a stubbly beard covered the haggard cheeks, across one of which was an ugly scratch. Yet the girl seemed to find it beautiful. Her eyes filled with tears as she gazed at it; she brushed back a lock of hair that had fallen over the forehead, and bent as though to press a kiss there—but stopped, with a quick shake of the head, and drew away.

" Not yet!" she whispered. " Not yet!" and crawling a little way apart, she lay down again among the bushes.

Again Stewart awoke with the sun in his eyes, and after a moment's confused blinking, he looked around to find himself alone.

The dull pain in his shoulder as he sat up reminded him of his wound. Crawling a little distance back among the bushes, he slipped out of his coat.

His shirt was soaked with blood half-way down the right side—a good sign, Stewart told himself. He knew how great a show a little blood can make, and he was glad that the wound had bled freely. He unbuttoned his shirt and gingerly pulled it back from the shoulder, for the blood had dried in places and stuck fast; then he removed the folded handkerchief, and the wound lay revealed.

He could just see it by twisting his head around, and he regarded it with satisfaction, for, as he had thought, it was not much more than a scratch. A bullet had grazed the shoulder-bone, plowed through the muscle and sped on its way, leaving behind, as the only sign of its passage, a tiny black mark.

" You are wounded! " cried a strangled voice, and in an instant his comrade was on her knees beside him, her face pale, her lips working. "And you did not tell me! Oh, cruel, cruel! "

There was that in the voice, in the eyes, in the trembling lips which sent Stewart's heart leaping into his throat. But, by a mighty effort, he kept his arms from around her.

"Nonsense! " he said, as lightly as he could. " That's not a wound—it is just a scratch. This one across my cheek hurts a blamed sight worse! If I could only wash it——"

"There is a little stream back yonder," she said, and sprang to her feet. "Come! Or perhaps you cannot walk!" and she put her arms around him to help him up.

He rose with a laugh.

"Really," he protested, "I don't see how a scratch on the shoulder could affect my legs!"

But she refused to make a jest of it.

"The blood—it frightens me. Are you very weak?" she asked, anxiously, holding tight to him, as though he might collapse at any instant.

"If I am," said Stewart, "it is from want of food, not from loss of blood. I haven't lost a spoonful. Ah, here's the brook!"

He knelt beside it, while she washed the blood from his handkerchief and tenderly bathed the injured shoulder. Stewart watched her with fast-beating heart. Surely she cared; surely there was more than friendly concern in that white face, in those quivering lips. Well, very soon now, he could put it to the touch. He trembled at the thought: would he win or lose?

"Am I hurting you?" she asked, anxiously, for she had felt him quiver.

"Not a bit—the cool water feels delightful. You see it is only a scratch," he added, when the clotted blood had been cleared away. "It will be quite well in two or three days. I sha'n't even have a scar! I think it might have left a scar! What's the use of being wounded, if one hasn't a scar to show for it? And I shall probably never be under fire again!"

She smiled wanly, and a little color crept back into her face.

"How you frightened me!" she said. "I came through the bushes and saw you sitting there, all covered with blood! You might have told me—it was foolish to lie there all night without binding it up. Suppose you had bled to death!" and she wrung out the handkerchief, shook it out in the breeze until it was nearly dry, and bound it tightly over the wound. "How does that feel?"

"It feels splendid! Really it does," he added, seeing that she regarded him doubtfully. "If I feel the least little twinge of pain, I will notify you instantly. I give you my word!"

They sat for a moment silent, gazing into each other's eyes. It was the girl who stirred first.

"I will go to the edge of the wood and reconnoiter," she said, rising a little unsteadily, "while you wash your hands and face. Or shall I stay and help?"

"No," said Stewart, "thank you. I think I am

still able to wash my own face—that is, if you think it's any use to wash it!" and he ran his fingers along his stubbly jaws. "Do you think you will like me with a beard?"

"With a beard or without one, it is all the same!" she answered, softly, and slipped quickly away among the trees, leaving Stewart to make what he could of this cryptic utterance.

Despite his gnawing hunger, despite his stiff shoulder and sore muscles, he was very, very happy as he bent above the clear water and drank deep, and bathed hands and face. How good it was to be alive! How good it was to be just here this glorious morning! With no man on earth would he have changed places!

He did not linger over his toilet. Every moment away from his comrade was a moment lost. He found her sitting at the edge of the wood, gazing down across the valley, her hair stirring slightly in the breeze, her whole being radiant with youth. He looked at her for a moment, and then he looked down at himself.

"What a scarecrow I am," he said, and ruefully contemplated a long tear in his coat—merely the largest of half a dozen. "And I lost my collar in that dash last night—I left it on the bank, and didn't dare stop to look for it. Even if we met the Germans now, there would be no danger—they would take us for tramps!"

"I know I look like a scarecrow," she laughed; "but you might have spared telling me!"

"You!" cried Stewart. "A scarecrow! Oh, no; you would attract the birds. They would find you adorable!"

His eyes added that not alone to the birds was she adorable.

She cast one glance at him—a luminous glance, shy yet glad; abashed yet rejoicing. Then she turned away.

"There is a village over yonder," she said. "We can get something to eat there, and find out where we are. Listen! What is that?"

Away to the south a dull rumbling shook the horizon—a mighty shock as of an earthquake.

"The Germans have got their siege-guns into position," he said. "They are attacking Liège again."

Yes, there could be no doubt of it; murder and desolation were stalking across the country to the south. But nothing could be more peaceful than the fields which stretched before them.

"There is no danger here," said Stewart, and led the way down across the rough pasture to the road.

As he mounted the wall, moved by some strange uneasiness, he stopped to look back toward the east; but the road stretched white and empty until it plunged into a strip of woodland a mile away.

Somehow he was not reassured. With that strange uneasiness still weighing on him, a sense of oppression as of an approaching storm, he sprang down beside the girl, and they set off westward side by side. At first they could not see the village, which was hid by a spur of rising ground; then, at a turn of the road, they found it close in front of them.

But the road was blocked with fallen trees, strung with barbed wire—and what was that queer embankment of fresh, yellow earth which stretched to right and left?

"The Belgians!" cried the girl. "Come! We are safe at last!" and she started to run forward.

But only for an instant. As though that cry of hers was an awaited signal, there came a crash of musketry from the wooded ridge to the right, and an answering crash from the crest of the embankment; and Stewart saw that light and speeding figure spin half round, crumple in upon itself, and drop limply to the road.

CHAPTER XV

DISASTER

HE was beside her in an instant, his arm around her, raising her. He scarcely heard the guns; he scarcely heard the whistle of the bullets; he knew only, as he knelt there in the road, that his little comrade had been stricken down.

Where was she wounded?

Not in the head, thank God! Not in the throat, so white and delicate. The breast, perhaps, and with trembling fingers he tore aside the coat.

She opened her eyes and looked dazedly up at him.

"*Qu'y a-t-il?*" she murmured. Then her vision cleared. "What is the matter?" she asked in a stronger voice.

"You've been hit," he panted. "Do you feel pain?"

She closed her eyes for an instant.

"No," she answered; "but my left leg is numb, as if——"

"Pray heaven it is only in the leg! I must get you somewhere out of this." He raised his head to look around, and was suddenly conscious of the banging guns. "Damn these lunatics! Oh, damn them!"

The ridges on either side were rimmed with fire. He cast a glance behind him and his heart stood still, for a troop of cavalry was deploying into the road. Forward, then, to the village, since that was the only way.

He stooped to lift her.

"I may hurt you a little," he said.

"What are you going to do?"

"I'm going to carry you to the village. Here, wave your handkerchief to show them that we are friends," and he drew it from her pocket and thrust it into her hand. "Now, your arm about my neck."

She obeyed mutely; then, as he straightened up, she saw, over his shoulder, the cavalry forming for the charge.

"No, no!" she cried. "Put me down. Here are the letters! See, I am placing them in your pocket! Now, put me down and save yourself!"

He was picking his way forward over the barbed wire. He dared not lift his eyes from the road even for a glance at her.

"Be still!" he commanded. "Don't struggle so! I will not put you down! Wave the handkerchief!"

"There is cavalry down yonder," she protested, wildly. "It will charge in a moment!"

"I know it! That's one reason I will not put you down!"

He was past the wire; he could look at her for an instant—into her eyes, so close to his; deep into her eyes, dark with fear and pain.

"Another reason is," he said, deliberately, "that I love you! I am telling you now because I want you to know, if this should be the end! I love you, love you, love you!"

He was forced to look away from her, for there were fallen trees in front, but he felt the arm around his neck tighten.

And then he bent his head and kissed her.

"Like that!" he said, hoarsely. "Only a thousand times more than that—a million times more than that!"

She pulled herself up until her cheek was pressed to his; and her eyes were like twin stars.

"And I!" she whispered. "A million times more than that. Oh, my prince, my lover!"

Stewart's veins ran fire. His fatigue dropped from him. He trod on air. He threw back his head proudly, for he felt himself invincible. He was contemptuous of fate—it could not harm him now!

"And yet you wanted me to put you down!" he mocked.

She snuggled against him, warm and womanly; she gave herself to him.

"Oh, hold me close!" she seemed to say. "Hold me close, close! I am yours now!"

"Wave the handkerchief!" he added. "We're getting near the barricade. Life is too sweet to end just yet!"

She smiled up into his eyes, and waved the handkerchief at arm's length above their heads. Stewart, glancing up, saw a row of faces crowned by queer black shakos peering curiously down from the top of the barricade.

"They have seen us!" he said. "They're not firing! They understand that we are friends! Courage, little comrade!"

"I am not afraid," she smiled. "And I love that name—little comrade!"

"Here are the last entanglements—and then we're through. What is that cavalry doing?"

She gave a little cry as she looked back along the road. At the same instant, Stewart heard the thunder of galloping hoofs.

"They are coming!" she screamed. "Oh, put me down! Put me down!"

"Not I!" gasped Stewart between his teeth, and glanced over his shoulder.

The Uhlans were charging in solid mass, their lances couched.

There was just one chance of escape—Stewart saw it instantly. Holding the girl close, he leaped into the ditch beside the road and threw himself flat against the ground, shielding her with his body.

In an instant the thunder of the charge was upon him. Then, high above the rattle of guns, rose the shouts of men, the screams of horses, the savage shock of the encounter. Something rolled upon him,—lay quivering against him—a wounded man—a dead one, perhaps—in any event, he told himself, grimly, so much added protection. Pray heaven that a maddened horse did not tramp them down!

The tumult died, the firing slackened. What was that? A burst of cheering?

Stewart ventured to raise his head and look about him; then, with a gasp, he threw off the weight, caught up his companion and staggered to his feet. Yes; it was a body which had fallen upon him. It rolled slowly over on its back as he arose, and he saw a ghastly wound between the eyes.

"They have been repulsed!" he panted. "Wave the handkerchief!" With his heart straining in his throat, he clambered out of the ditch and staggered on. "Don't look!" he added, for the road was strewn with horrors. "Don't look!"

She gazed up at him, smiling calmly.

"I shall look only at you, my lover!" she said, softly, and Stewart tightened his grip and held her close!

There was the barricade, with cheering men atop it, exposing themselves with utter recklessness to the bullets which still whistled from right and left. Stewart felt his knees trembling. Could he reach it? Could he lift his foot over this entanglement? Could he possibly step across this body?

Suddenly he felt his burden lifted from him and a strong arm thrown about his shoulders.

"Friends!" he gasped. "We're friends!"

Then he heard the girl's clear voice speaking in rapid French, and men's voices answering eagerly. The mist cleared a little from before his eyes, and he found that the arm about his shoulders belonged to a stocky Belgian soldier who was leading him past one end of the barricade, close behind another who bore the girl in his arms.

At the other side an officer stopped them.

"Who are you?" he asked in French. "From where do you come?"

"We are friends," said the girl. "We have fled from Germany. We have both been wounded."

"Yes," said Stewart, and showed his blood-stained shirt. "Mine is only a scratch, but my comrade needs attention."

A sudden shout from the top of the barricade told that the Uhlans were re-forming.

"You must look out for yourselves," said the officer. "I will hear your story later," and he bounded back to his place beside his men.

The soldier who was carrying the girl dropped her abruptly into Stewart's arms and followed his captain. In an instant the firing recommenced.

Stewart looked wildly about him. He was in a village street, with close-built houses on either side.

"I must find a wagon," he gasped, "or something——"

His breath failed him, but he staggered on. The mist was before his eyes again, his tongue seemed dry and swollen.

Suddenly the arm about his neck relaxed, the head fell back——

He cast one haggard glance down into the white face, then turned through the nearest doorway.

Perhaps she was wounded more seriously than he had thought—perhaps she had not told him. He must see—he must make sure——

He found himself in a tiled passage, opening into a low-ceilinged room lighted by a single window. For an instant, in the semi-darkness, he stared blindly; then he saw a low settle against the farther wall, and upon this he gently laid his burden.

Before he could catch himself, he had fallen heavily to the floor, and lay there for a moment, too weak to rise. But the weakness passed. With set teeth, he pulled himself to his knees, got out his knife, found, with his fingers, the stain of blood above the wound in the leg, and quickly ripped away the cloth.

The bullet had passed through the thickness of the thigh, leaving a tiny puncture. With a sob of thankfulness, he realized that the wound was not dangerous. Blood was still oozing slowly from it— it must be washed and dressed.

He found a pail of water in the kitchen, snatched a sheet from a bed in another room, and set to work. The familiar labor steadied him, the mists cleared, his muscles again obeyed his will, the sense of exhaustion passed.

" It is only a scratch ! " whispered a voice, and he

turned sharply to find her smiling up at him.   " It
is just a scratch like yours ! "

" It is much more than a scratch ! " he said,
sternly.   " You must lie still, or you will start the
bleeding."

" Tyrant ! " she retorted, and then she raised her
head and looked to see what he was doing.   " Oh !
is it there? " she said, in surprise.   " I didn't feel it
there ! "

" Where did you feel it ? " Stewart demanded,
" Not in the body?   Tell me the truth ! "

" It seemed to me to be somewhere below the knee.
But how savage you are ! "

" I'm savage because you are hurt.   I can't stand
it to see you suffer ! " and with lips compressed, he
bandaged the wound with some strips torn from the
sheet.   Then he ran his fingers down over the calf,
and brought them away stained with blood.   He
caught up his knife and ripped the cloth clear down.

" Really," she protested, " I shall not have any
clothing left, if you keep on like that !   I do not see
how I am going to appear in public as it is ! "

He grimly washed the blood away without replying.   On either side of the calf, he found a tiny
black spot where the second bullet had passed
through.

"These German bullets seem to be about the size of peas," he remarked, as he bandaged the leg; then he raised his head and listened, as the firing outside rose to a furious crescendo. "They're at it again!" he added. "We must be getting out of this!"

She reached up, caught him by the coat, and drew him down to her.

"Listen," she said. "The letters are in your pocket. Should we be separated——"

"We will not be separated," he broke in, impatiently. "Do you suppose I would permit anything to separate us now?"

"I know, dear one," she said, softly. "But if we should be, you will carry the letters to General Joffre? Oh, do not hesitate!" she cried. "Promise me! They mean so much to me—my life's work —all my ambitions—all my hopes——"

"Very well," he said. "I promise."

"You have not forgotten the sign and the formula?"

"No."

She passed an arm about his neck and drew him still closer.

"Kiss me!" she whispered.

And Stewart, shaken, transported, deliriously

happy, pressed his lips to hers in a long, close, passionate embrace.

At last she drew her arm away.

" I am very tired," she whispered, smiling dreamily up at him; "and very, very happy. I do not believe I can go on, dear one."

" I will get a wagon of some kind—a hand-cart, if nothing better. There must be ambulances somewhere about——"

He paused, listening, for the firing at the barricade had started furiously again.

" I will be back in a moment," he said, and ran to the street door and looked out. As he did so, a wounded soldier hobbled past, using his rifle as a crutch.

" How goes it? " Stewart inquired, in French.

" We hold them off," answered the soldier, smiling cheerfully, though his face was drawn with pain.

" Will they break through? "

" No. Our reënforcements are coming up," and the little soldier hobbled away down the street.

" I should have asked him where the ambulances are," thought Stewart. He glanced again toward the barricade. The firing had slackened; evidently the assailants had again been repulsed. Yes, there was time, and he darted down the street after the limping soldier. He was at his side in a moment. " Where are the ambulances? " he asked.

The soldier, turning to reply, glanced back along the street and his face went livid.

" Ah, good God! " he groaned. " Look yonder! "

And, looking, Stewart beheld a gray-green flood pouring over the barricade, beheld the flash of reddened bayonets, beheld the little band of Belgians swept backward.

With a cry of anguish, he sprang back along the street, but in an instant the tide was upon him. He fought against it furiously, striking, cursing, praying——

And suddenly he found himself face to face with the Belgian officer, blood-stained, demoniac, shouting encouragement to his men. His eyes flashed with amazement when he saw Stewart.

" Go back! Go back! " he shouted.

" My comrade is back there! " panted Stewart, and tried to pass.

But the officer caught his arm.

" Madman! " he cried. " It is death to go that way! "

" What is that to me? " retorted Stewart, and wrenched his arm away.

The officer watched him for an instant, then turned away with a shrug. After all, he reflected, it was none of his affair; his task was to hold the Germans back, and he threw himself into it.

"Steady, men!" he shouted. "Steady! Our reserves are coming!"

And his men cheered and held a firm front, though it cost them dear—so firm and steady that Stewart found he could not get past it, but was carried back foot by foot, too exhausted to resist, entangled hopelessly in the retreat. The Germans pressed forward, filling the street from side to side, compact, irresistible.

And then the Belgians heard behind them the gallop of horses, the roll of heavy wheels, and their captain, glancing back, saw that a quick-firer had swung into position in the middle of the street.

"Steady, men!" he shouted. "We have them now! Steady till I give the word!" He glanced back again and caught the gun-captain's nod. "Now! To the side and back!" he screamed.

The men, with a savage cheer, sprang to right and left, into doorways, close against the walls, and the gun, with a purr of delight, let loose its lightnings into the advancing horde.

Stewart, who had been swept aside with the

others without understanding what was happening, gasping, rubbing his eyes, staring down the street, saw the gray line suddenly stop and crumple up. Then, with a savage yell, it dashed forward and stopped again. He saw an officer raise his sword to urge them on, then fall crashing to the street; he saw that instant of indecision which is fatal to any charge; and then stark terror ran through the ranks, and they turned to flee.

But the pressure from the rear cut off escape in that direction, and the human flood burst into the houses on either side, swept through them, out across the fields, and away. And steadily the little gun purred on, as though reveling in its awful work, until the street was clear.

But the Germans, though they had suffered terribly, were not yet routed. A remnant of them held together behind the houses at the end of the street, and still others took up a position behind the barricade and swept the street with their rifles.

The little officer bit his lip in perplexity as he looked about at his company, so sadly reduced in numbers. Should he try to retake the barricade with a rush, or should he wait for reënforcements? He loved his men—surely, they had more than played their part. Then his eye was caught by a bent figure which dodged from doorway to doorway.

"That madman again!" he muttered, and watched, expecting every instant to see him fall.

For Stewart had not waited for the captain's decision. Almost before the Germans turned to flee, he was creeping low along the wall, taking advantage of such shelter as there was. The whistle of the machine-gun's bullets filled the street. One nipped him across the wrist, another grazed his arm, and then, as the Germans rallied, he saw ahead of him the vicious flashes of their rifles.

He was not afraid; indeed, he was strangely calm. He was quite certain that he would not be killed— others might fall, but not he. Others—yes, here they were; dozens, scores, piled from wall to wall. For here was where the machine-gun had caught the German advance and smote it down. They lay piled one upon another, young men, all of them; some lying with arms flung wide, staring blindly up at the sky; a few moaning feebly, knowing only that they suffered; two or three trying to pull themselves from beneath the heap of dead; one coward burrowing deeper into it! He could hear the thud, thud of the bullets from either end of the street as they struck the mass of bodies, dead and wounded alike, until there were no longer any wounded; until even the coward lay still!

Sick and dizzy, he pushed on. Was this the house? The door stood open and he stepped inside and looked around. No, this was not it.

The next one, perhaps—all these houses looked alike from the street. As he reached the door, a swirl of acrid smoke beat into his face. He looked out quickly. The barricade was obscured by smoke; dense masses rolled out of the houses on either side. The Germans had fired the village!

Into the next house Stewart staggered—vainly; and into the next. He could hear the crackling of the flames; the smoke grew thicker——

Into the next!

He knew it the instant he crossed the threshold; yes, this was the entry, this was the room, there was the settle——

He stopped, staring, gasping——

The settle was empty.

Slowly he stepped forward, gazing about him. Yes, there was the bucket of water on the floor, just as he had left it; there were the blood-stained rags; there was the torn sheet.

But the settle was empty.

He threw himself beside it and ran his hands over it, to be sure that his eyes were not deceiving him.

No; the settle was empty.

He ran into the next room and the next. He ran all through the house calling, " Comrade! Little comrade!"

But there was no reply. The rooms were empty, one and all.

Half-suffocated, palsied with despair, he reeled back to the room where he had left her, and stared about it. Could he be mistaken? No; there was the bucket, the bandages——

But what was that dark stain in the middle of the white, sanded floor. He drew close and looked at it. It was blood.

Still staring, he backed away. Blood—whose blood? Not hers! Not his little comrade's!

And suddenly his strength fell from him; he staggered, dropped to his knees——

This was the end, then—this was the end. There on the settle was where she had lain; it was there she had drawn him down for that last caress; and the letters,—ah, they would never be delivered now! But at least he could die there, with his head where hers had been.

Blinded, choking, he dragged himself forward—here was the place!

" Little comrade! " he murmured. " Little comrade! "

And he fell forward across the settle, his face buried in his arms.

CHAPTER XVI

A TRUST FULFILLED

WHEN Stewart opened his eyes again it was to find himself looking up into a good-humored face, which he did not at first recognize. It was brown and dirty, there was a three-days' growth of beard upon cheeks and chin, and a deep red scratch across the forehead, but the eyes were bright and the lips smiling, as of a man superior to every fortune—and then he recognized the little Belgian captain whose troops had defended the village.

Instantly memory surged back upon him—memory bitter and painful. He raised his head and looked about him. He was lying under a clump of trees not far from the bank of a little stream, along which a company of Belgian soldiers were busy throwing up intrenchments.

"Ah, so you are better!" said the captain, in his clipped French, his eyes beaming with satisfaction. "That is good! A little more of that smoke, and it would have been all over with you!" and he gestured toward the eastern horizon, above which hung a black and threatening cloud.

Stewart pulled himself to a sitting posture and stared for a moment at the cloud as it billowed in the wind. Then he passed his hand before his eyes and stared again. And suddenly all his strength seemed to go from him and he lay quietly down again.

"So bad as that!" said the officer, sympathetically, struck by the whiteness of his face. "And I have nothing to give you—not a swallow of wine—not a sip!"

"It will pass," said Stewart, hoarsely. "I shall be all right presently. But I do not understand French very well. Do you speak English?"

"A lit-tle," answered the other, and spoke thereafter in a mixture of French and English, which Stewart found intelligible, but which need not be indicated here.

"Will you tell me what happened?" Stewart asked, at last.

"Ah, we drove them out!" cried the captain, his face gleaming. "My men behaved splendidly—they are brave boys, as you yourself saw. We made it—how you say?—too hot for the Germans; but we could not remain. They were pushing up in force on every side, and they had set fire to the place. So we took up our wounded and fell back. At the last moment, I happen to remember that I had seen you dodging along the street in face of the German fire, so I look for you in this house and in that. At last I find you in a room full of smoke, lying across a bench, and I bring you away. Now we wait for another attack. It will come soon—our scouts have seen the Germans preparing to advance. Then we fight as long as we can and kill as many as we can, and then give back to a new position. That, over and over again, will be our part in this war—to hold them until France has time to strike. But I pity my poor country," and his face grew dark. "There will be little left of her when those barbarians have finished. They are astounded that we fight, that we dare oppose them; they are maddened that we hold them back, for time means everything to them. They revenge themselves by burning our villages and killing defenseless people. Ah, well, they shall pay! Tell me, my friend," he added, in another tone, "why did you risk death in that reckless fashion? Why did you kneel beside that bench?"

"It was there I left my comrade," Stewart answered, brokenly, his face convulsed. "She was wounded—she could not walk—I was too exhausted to carry her—I went to look for a cart—for an ambulance—I had scarcely taken a step, when the Germans swept over the barricade and into the town. When I got back to the house where I had left her, she was not there."

" Ah," said the other, looking down at Stewart, thoughtfully. " It was a woman, then? "

" Yes."

" Your wife? "

" She had promised to become my wife," and Stewart looked at the other, steadily.

" You are an American, are you not? "

" Yes—I have my passport."

" And Madame—was she also an American? "

" No—she was a Frenchwoman. She was shot twice in the leg as we ran toward your barricade— seriously—it was quite impossible for her to walk. But when I got back to the house, she was not there. What had happened to her? "

His companion gazed out over the meadows and shook his head.

" You looked in the other rooms? " he asked.

" Everywhere—all through the house—she was not there! Ah, and I remember now," he added, struggling to a sitting posture, his face more livid, if possible, than it had been before. " There was a great bloodstain on the floor that was not there when I left her. How could it have got there? I cannot understand!"

Again the officer shook his head, his eyes still on the billowing smoke.

" It is very strange," he murmured.

" I must go back!" cried Stewart. " I must search for her!" and he tried to rise.

The other put out a hand to stop him, but drew it back, seeing it unnecessary.

" Impossible!" he said. " You see, you cannot even stand!"

" I have had nothing to eat since yesterday," Stewart explained. " Then only some eggs and apples. If I could get some food——"

He broke off, his chin quivering helplessly, as he realized his weakness. He was very near to tears.

" Even if you could walk," the other pointed out, " even if you were quite strong, it would still be impossible. The Germans have burned the village; they are now on this side of it. If Madame is still alive, she is safe. Barbarians as they are, they would not kill a wounded woman!"

" Oh, you don't know!" groaned Stewart. " You don't know! They would kill her without compunction!" and weakness and hunger and despair were too much for him. He threw himself forward on his face, shaken by great sobs.

The little officer sat quite still, his face very sad. There was no glory about war—that was merely a fiction to hold soldiers to their work; it was all horrible, detestable, inhuman. He had seen brave men killed, torn, mutilated; he had seen inoffensive people driven from their homes and left to starve; he had seen women weeping for their husbands and children for their fathers; he had seen terror stalk across the quiet countryside—famine, want, despair——

The paroxysm passed, and Stewart gradually regained his self-control.

"You will, of course, do as you think best," said his companion, at last; "but I could perhaps be of help if I knew more. How do you come to be in these rags? Why was Madame dressed as a man? Why should the Germans kill her? These are things that I should like to know—but you will tell me as much or as little as you please."

Before he was well aware of it, so hungry was he for comfort, Stewart found himself embarked upon the story. It flowed from his lips so rapidly, so brokenly, as poignant memory stabbed through him, that more than once his listener stopped him and asked him to repeat. For the rest, he sat staring out at the burning village, his eyes bright, his hands clenched.

And when the story was over, he arose, faced the east, and saluted stiffly.

"*Madame!*" he said—and so paid her the highest tribute in a soldier's power.

Then he sat down again, and there was a moment's silence.

"What you have told me," he said, slowly, at last, "moves me beyond words! Believe me, I would advance this instant, I would risk my whole command, if I thought there was the slightest chance of rescuing that intrepid and glorious woman. But there is no chance. That village is held by at least a regiment."

"What could have happened?" asked Stewart, again. "Where could she have gone?"

"I cannot imagine. I can only hope that she is safe. Most probably she has been taken prisoner. Even in that case, there is little danger that she will ever be recognized."

"But why should they take prisoner a wounded civilian?" Stewart persisted. "I cannot understand it—unless——"

His voice died in his throat.

"Unless what?" asked the officer, turning on him quickly. "What is it you fear?"

"Unless she *was* recognized!" cried Stewart, hoarsely.

But the other shook his head.

"If she had been recognized—which is most improbable—she would not have been taken prisoner at all. She would have been shot where she lay."

And then again that dark stain upon the floor flashed before Stewart's eyes. Perhaps that had really happened. Perhaps that blood was hers!

"It is the suspense!" he groaned. "The damnable suspense!"

"I know," said the other, gently. "It is always the missing who cause the deepest anguish. One can only wait and hope and pray! That is all that you can do—that and one other thing."

"What other thing?" Stewart demanded.

"She intrusted you with a mission, did she not?" asked the little captain, gently. "Living or dead, she would be glad to know that you fulfilled it, for it was very dear to her. You still have the letters?"

Stewart thrust his hand into his pocket and brought them forth.

"You are right," he said, and rose unsteadily. "Where will I find General Joffre?"

The other had risen, too, and was supporting him with a strong hand.

"That I do not know," he answered; "somewhere along the French frontier, no doubt, mustering his forces."

Stewart looked about him uncertainly.

"If I were only stronger," he began.

"Wait," the little officer broke in. "I think I have it—I am expecting instructions from our headquarters at St. Trond—they should arrive at any moment—and I can send you back in the car which brings them. At headquarters they will be able to tell you something definite, and perhaps to help you." He glanced anxiously toward the east and then cast an appraising eye over the intrenchments his troops had dug. "We can hold them back for a time," he added, "but we need reënforcements badly. Ah, there comes the car!"

A powerful gray motor spun down the road from the west, kicking up a great cloud of dust, and in a moment the little captain had received his instructions. He tore the envelope open and read its contents eagerly. Then he turned to his men, his face shining.

"The Sixty-third will be here in half an hour!"
he shouted. "We will give those fellows a hot dose
this time!"

His men cheered the news with waving shakos,
then, with a glance eastward, fell to work again on
their trenches, which would have to be extended to
accommodate the reënforcements. Their captain
stepped close to the side of the purring car, made his
report to an officer who sat beside the driver, and
then the two carried on for a moment a low-toned
conversation. More than once they glanced at Stewart, and the conversation ended with a sharp nod
from the officer in the car. The other came hurrying back.

"It is all right," he said. "You will be at St.
Trond in half an hour," and he helped him to mount
into the tonneau.

For an instant Stewart stood there, staring back
at the cloud of smoke above the burning village;
then he dropped into the seat and turned to say
good-by to the gallant fellow who had proved so
true a friend.

The little soldier was standing with heels together,
head thrown back, hand at the visor of his cap.

"*Monsieur!*" he said, simply, as his eyes met
Stewart's, and then the car started.

Stewart looked back through a mist of tears, and waved his hand to that martial little figure, so hopeful and indomitable. Should he ever see that gallant friend again? Chance was all against it. An hour hence, he might be lying in the road, a bullet through his heart; if not an hour hence, then tomorrow or next day. And before this war was over, how many others would be lying so, arms flung wide, eyes staring at the sky—just as those young Germans had lain back yonder!

He thrust such thoughts away. They were too bitter, too terrible. But as his vision cleared, he saw on every hand the evidence of war's desolation.

The road was thronged with fugitives—old men, women, and children—fleeing westward away from their ruined homes, away from the plague which was devastating their land. Their faces were vacant with despair, or wet with silent tears. For whither could they flee? Where could they hope for food and shelter? How could their journey end, save at the goal of death?

The car threaded its way slowly among these heart-broken people, passed through silent and deserted villages, by fields of grain that would never be harvested, along quiet streams which would soon be red with blood; and at last it came to St. Trond, and stopped before the town-hall, from whose beautiful old belfry floated the Belgian flag.

"If you will wait here, sir," said the officer, and jumped to the pavement and hurried up the steps.

So Stewart waited, an object of much curiosity to the passing crowd. Other cars dashed up from time to time, officers jumped out with reports, jumped in again with orders and dashed away. Plainly, Belgium was not dismayed even in face of this great invasion. She was fighting coolly, intelligently, with her whole strength.

And then an officer came down the steps, sprang to the footboard of the machine, and looked at Stewart.

"I am told you have a message," he said.

"Yes."

"I am a member of the French staff. Can you deliver it to me?"

"I was told to deliver it only to General Joffre."

"Ah! in that case——"

The officer caught his lower lip between the thumb and little finger of his left hand, as if in perplexity. So naturally was it done that for an instant Stewart did not recognize the sign; then, hastily, he passed his left hand across his eyes.

The officer looked at him keenly.

" Have we not met before? " he asked.

" In Berlin; on the twenty-second," Stewart answered.

The officer's face cleared, and he stepped over the door into the tonneau.

" I am at your service, sir," he said. " First you must rest a little, and have some clean clothes, and a bath and food. I can see that you have had a hard time. Then we will set out."

An hour later, more comfortable in body than it had seemed possible he could ever be again, Stewart lay back among the deep cushions of a high-powered car, which whizzed southward along a pleasant road. He did not know his destination. He had not inquired, and indeed he did not care. But had he known Belgium, he would have recognized Landen and Ramillies; he would have known that those high white cliffs ahead bordered the Meuse; he would have seen that this pinnacled town they were approaching was Namur.

The car was stopped at the city gate by a sentry, and taken to the town-hall, where the chauffeur's papers were examined and verified. Then they were off again, across the placid river and straight southward, close beside its western bank. Stewart had never seen a more beautiful country. The other shore was closed in by towering rugged cliffs, with a white villa here and there squeezed in between wall and water or perched on a high ledge. Sometimes the cliffs gave back to make room for a tiny, red-roofed village; again they were riven by great fissures or pitted with yawning chasms.

Evening came, and still the car sped southward. There were no evidences here of war. As the calm stars came out one by one, Stewart could have fancied that it was all a dream, but for that dull agony of the spirit which he felt would never leave him—and for that strand of lustrous hair which now lay warm above his heart—and which, alas! was all he had of her!

Yes—there were the two letters which rustled under his fingers as he thrust them into his pocket. He had looked at them more than once during the afternoon, delighting to handle them because they had been hers, imagining that he could detect on them the faint aroma of her presence. He had turned them over and over, had slipped out the sheets of closely-written paper, and read them through and through, hoping for some clew to the identity of the woman he had lost. It was an added anguish that he did not even know her name!

The letters did not help him. They contained

nothing but innocent, careless, light-hearted, impersonal gossip, written apparently by one young woman to another. " My dear cousin," they were addressed, and Stewart could have wept at the irony which denied him even her first name. They were in English—excellent English—a little stiff, perhaps —just such English as she had spoken—and the envelopes bore the superscription, " Mrs. Bradford Stewart, Spa, Belgium." But so far as he could see they had nothing to do with her—they were just a part of the elaborate plot in which he had been entangled.

But what secret could they contain? A code? If so, it was very perfect, for nothing could be more simple, more direct, more unaffected than the letters themselves. A swift doubt swept over him. Perhaps, once in the presence of the general, he would find that he had played the fool—that there was nothing in these letters.

And yet a woman had risked her life for them. Face to face with death, she had made him swear to deliver them. Well, he would keep his oath!

He was still very tired, and at last he lay back. among the cushions and closed his eyes and tried to sleep.

"*Halte là!*" cried a sharp voice.

The brakes squeaked and groaned as they were jammed down. Stewart, shaken from his nap, sat up and looked about him. Ahead gleamed the lights of a town; he could hear a train rumbling past along the river bank.

There was a moment's colloquy between the chauffeur and a man in uniform; a paper was examined by the light of an electric torch; then the man stepped to one side and the car started slowly ahead.

The rumbling train came to a stop, and Stewart, rubbing his eyes, saw a regiment of soldiers leaping from it down to a long, brilliantly-lighted platform. They wore red trousers and long blue coats folded back in front—and with a shock, Stewart realized that they were French—that these were the men who were soon to face those gray-clad legions back yonder. Then, above the entrance to the station, its name flashed into view,—"Givet." They had passed the frontier—they were in France.

The car rolled on, crossed the river by a long bridge, and finally came to a stop before a great, barn-like building, every window of which blazed with light, and where streams of officers were constantly arriving and departing.

At once a sentry leaped upon the footboard; again

the chauffeur produced his paper, and an officer was summoned, who glanced at it, and immediately stepped back and threw open the door of the tonneau.

" This way, sir, if you please," he said to Stewart.

As the latter rose heavily, stiff with long sitting, the officer held out his arm and helped him to alight.

" You are very tired, is it not so? " he asked, and still supporting him, led the way up the steps, along a hall, and into a long room where many persons were sitting on benches against the walls or slowly walking up and down. " You will wait here," added his guide. " It will not be long," and he hurried away.

Stewart dropped upon a bench and looked about him. There were a few women in the room—and he wondered at their presence there—but most of its occupants were men, some in uniform, others in civilian dress of the most diverse kinds, of all grades of society. Stewart was struck at once by the fact that they were all silent, exchanging not a word, not even a glance. Each kept his eyes to himself as if it were a point of honor so to do.

Suddenly Stewart understood. These were agents of the secret service, waiting to report to their chief or to be assigned to some difficult and dangerous task. One by one they were summoned, disappeared through the door, and did not return.

At last it was to Stewart the messenger came.

"This way, sir," he said.

Stewart followed him out into the hall, through a door guarded by two sentries, and into a little room beyond a deep ante-chamber, where a white-haired man sat before a great table covered with papers. The messenger stood aside for Stewart to pass, then went swiftly out and closed the door.

The man at the table examined his visitor with a long and penetrating glance, his face cold, impassive, expressionless.

"You are not one of ours," he said, at last, in English.

"No, I am an American."

"So I perceived. And yet you have a message?"

"Yes."

"How came you by it?"

"It was intrusted to me by one of your agents who joined me at Aix-la-Chapelle."

A sudden flame of excitement blazed into the cold eyes.

"May I ask your name?"

"Bradford Stewart."

The man snatched up a memorandum from the

desk and glanced at it. Then he sprang to his feet.

" Your pardon, Mr. Stewart," he said. " I did not catch your name—or, if I did, my brain did not supply the connection, as it should have done. My only excuse is that I have so many things to think of. Pray sit down," and he drew up a chair. " Where is the person who joined you at Aix? "

" I fear that she is dead," answered Stewart, in a low voice.

" Dead! " echoed the other, visibly and deeply moved. " Dead! But no, that cannot be! " He passed his hand feverishly before his eyes. " I will hear your story presently—first, the message. It is a written one? "

" Yes, in the form of two letters."

" May I see them? "

Stewart hesitated.

" I promised to deliver them only to General Joffre," he explained.

" I understand. But the general is very busy. I must see the letters for a moment before I ask him for an audience."

Without a word, Stewart passed them over. He saw the flush of excitement with which the other looked at them; he saw how his hand trembled as he drew out the sheets, glanced at them, thrust them hastily back, and touched a button on his desk.

Instantly the door opened and the messenger appeared.

" Inquire of General Joffre if he can see me for a moment on a matter of the first importance," said the man. The messenger bowed and withdrew. " Yes, of the first importance," he added, turning to Stewart, with shining eyes. " Here are the letters— I will not deprive you, sir, of the pleasure of yourself placing them in our general's hands. And it is to him you shall tell your story."

The door opened and the messenger appeared.

" The general will be pleased to receive Monsieur at once," he said, and stood aside for them to pass.

At the end of the hall was a large room crowded with officers. Beyond this was a smaller room where six men, each with his secretary, sat around a long table. At its head sat a plump little man, with white hair and bristling white mustache, which contrasted strongly with a face darkened and reddened by exposure to wind and rain, and lighted by a pair of eyes incredibly bright.

He was busy with a memorandum, but looked up as Stewart and his companion entered.

" Well, Fernande? " he said; but Stewart did not

know till afterward that the man at his side was the famous head of the French Intelligence Department, the eyes and ears of the French army—captain of an army of his own, every member of which went daily in peril of a dreadful death.

"General," said Fernande, in a voice whose trembling earnestness caused every man present suddenly to raise his head, "I have the pleasure of introducing to you an American, Mr. Bradford Stewart, who, at great peril to himself, has brought you a message which I believe to be of the first importance."

General Joffre bowed.

"I am pleased to meet Mr. Stewart," he said. "What is this message?"

"It is in these letters, sir," said Stewart, and placed the envelopes in his hand.

The general glanced at them, then slowly drew out the enclosures.

"We shall need a candle," said Fernande; "also a flat dish of water."

One of the secretaries hastened away to get them. He was back in a moment, and Fernande, having lighted the candle, took from his waistcoat pocket a tiny phial of blue liquid, and dropped three drops into the dish.

"Now we are ready, gentlemen," he said. "You are about to witness a most interesting experiment."

He picked up one of the sheets, dipped it into the water, then held it close to the flame of the candle.

Stewart, watching curiously, saw a multitude of red lines leap out upon the sheet—lines which zigzagged this way and that, apparently without meaning.

But to the others in the room they seemed anything but meaningless. As sheet followed sheet, the whole staff crowded around the head of the table, snatching them up, holding them to the light, bending close to decipher minute writing. Their eyes were shining with excitement, their hands were trembling; they spoke in broken words, in bits of sentences.

"The enceinte——"

"Oh, a new bastion here at the left——"

"I thought so——"

"Three emplacements——"

"But this wall is simply a mask—it would present no difficulties——"

"This position could be flanked——"

It was the general himself who spoke the final word.

"This is the weak spot," he pointed out, his finger upon the last sheet of all. Then he turned to Stewart, his eyes gleaming. "Monsieur," he said, "I will not conceal from you that these papers are, as Fernande guessed, of the very first importance. Will you tell us how they came into your possession?"

And Stewart, as briefly as might be, told the story —the meeting at Aix, the arrest at Herbesthal, the flight over the hills, the passage of the Meuse, the attack on the village—his voice faltering at the end despite his effort to control it.

At first, the staff had kept on with its examination of the plans, but first one and then another laid them down and listened.

For a moment after he had finished, they sat silent, regarding him. Then General Joffre rose slowly to his feet, and the members of his staff rose with him.

"Monsieur," he said, "I shall not attempt to tell you how your words have moved me; but on behalf of France I thank you; on her behalf I give you the highest honor which it is in her power to bestow." His hand went to his buttonhole and detached a tiny red ribbon. In a moment he had affixed it to Stewart's coat. "The Legion, monsieur!" he said, and he stepped back and saluted.

Stewart, a mist of tears before his eyes, his throat suddenly contracted, looked down at the decoration, gleaming on his lapel like a spot of blood.

"It is too much," he protested, brokenly. "I do not deserve——"

"It is the proudest order in the world, monsieur," broke in the general, "but it is not too much. You have done for France a greater thing than you perhaps imagine. Some day you will know. Not soon, I fear," and his face hardened. "We have other work to do before we can make use of these sheets of paper. You saw the German army?"

"Yes, sir; a part of it."

"It is well equipped?"

"It seemed to me irresistible," said Stewart. "I had never imagined such swarms of men, such tremendous cannon——"

"We have heard something of those cannon," broke in the general. "Are they really so tremendous?"

"I know nothing about cannon," answered Stewart; "but——" and he described as well as he could the three monsters he had seen rolling along the road toward Liège.

His hearers listened closely, asked a question or two——

"I thank you again," said the general, at last. "What you tell us is most interesting. Is there anything else that I can do for you? If there is, I pray you to command me."

Stewart felt himself shaken by a sudden convulsive trembling.

"If I could get some news," he murmured, brokenly, "of—of my little comrade."

General Joffre shot him a quick glance. His face softened, grew tender with comprehension.

"Fernande," he said.

Fernande bowed.

"Everything possible shall be done, my general," he said. "I promise it. We shall not be long without tidings."

"Thank you," said Stewart. "That is all, I think."

"And you?"

"I? Oh, what does it matter!" And then he turned, fired by a sudden remembrance of a great white tent, of loaded ambulances. "Yes—there is something I might do. I am a surgeon. Will France accept my services?"

"She is honored to do so," said the general,

quickly. " I will see that it is done. Until to-morrow—I will expect you," and he held out his hand, while the staff came to a stiff salute.

" Until to-morrow," repeated Stewart, and followed Fernande to the door.

As he passed out, he glanced behind him. The members of the staff were bending above those red-lined sheets, their faces shining with eagerness——

The officers in the outer room, catching sight of the red ribbon, saluted as he passed. The sentry in the hall came stiffly to attention.

But Stewart's heart was bitter. Honor! Glory! What were they worth to him alone and desolate——

" Monsieur! " It was Fernande's voice, low, vibrant with sympathy. " You will pardon me for what I am about to say—but I think I understand. It was not alone for France you did this thing—it was for that ' little comrade,' as you have called her, so brave, so loyal, so indomitable that my heart is at her feet. Is it not so? "

He came a step nearer and laid a tender hand on Stewart's arm.

" Do not despair, I beg of you, my friend. She is not dead—it is impossible that she should be dead! Fate could not be so cruel. With her you shared a

few glorious days of peril, of trial, and of ecstasy—
then you were whirled apart. But only for a time.
Somewhere, sometime, you will find her again,
awaiting you. I know it! I feel it!"

But it was no longer Fernande that Stewart heard
—it was another voice, subtle, delicate, out of the
unknown——

His bosom lifted with a deep, convulsive breath.

"You are right!" he whispered. "I, too, feel it!
Sometime—somewhere——"

And his trembling fingers sought that tress of
lustrous hair, warm above his heart.

Far away to the east, a sentry in the gray uniform of the German army paced slowly back and
forth before a great white house looking across a
terraced garden down upon the Meuse. Three days
before, it had been the beautiful and carefully-
ordered home of a wealthy Belgian; now it reeked
with the odor of ether and iodine. In the spa-
cious dining-room an operating-table had been installed, and a sterilizing apparatus simmered in one
corner. Along its halls and in every room rows of
white cots were ranged—and each cot had its bandaged occupant.

On the terrace overlooking the river, two sur-

geons, thoroughly weary after a hard day, sat smoking and talking in low tones. Within, a white-clad
nurse stole from cot to cot, assuring herself that all
was as well as might be.

In a tiny room on the upper floor, a single cot
had been placed. As the nurse stopped at its open
door and held aloft her night-lamp, her eyes caught
the gleam of other eyes, and she stepped quickly
forward.

" What is it? " she asked, softly. " Why are you
not asleep? You are not in pain? "

The patient—a mere lad he seemed of not more
than seventeen—smiled and shook his head.

" I do not know German," he said in French.

The nurse placed her cool hand upon the patient's
brow to assure herself that there was no access of
fever.

" I speak French a little," she said, painfully, in
that language. And then she hesitated. " Tell me,
Fräulein," she went on, after a moment, " how you
came to be wounded. We have wondered much."

" My brother and I were trying to get through
your lines to Brussels where our mother is," the
patient answered, readily, still smiling. " I slipped
on a suit of my brother's clothes, thinking to make
better progress. But we were too late. We were

caught between two fires when your men stormed that village."

Despite the smile, there was a shimmer of anxiety in the eyes she turned upon the nurse. It was a poor story; she realized that it would not bear scrutiny, that it would break down at the first question; but, fevered and racked with pain, she had been able to devise no better one.

The nurse, at least, accepted it unquestioningly.

"Ach, how terrible!" she commented. "And your brother—what of him?"

"When I was wounded, he carried me into a house, and then hastened away to look for a cart or wagon in which to place me. Before he could get back, your men had taken the village."

"Then he is safe at least!"

"Yes, I am sure of it."

"But he must think you dead! He will not know that you were saved! Ach, what anguish must be his!"

"Yes, he will suffer," agreed the wounded girl, in a low tone.

The eyes of the tender-hearted German woman were misty as she gazed down at her patient and sought for some word of comfort.

"But think of his joy when he finds that you are

not dead!" she urged. "To-morrow you shall give me his address and I will write. He will come for you, no doubt, as soon as he can."

"Yes, I am sure of that also!"

There was a subtle timbre in the voice that caught the nurse's ear, and she looked down again into the luminous eyes.

"You do not seem to mind your misfortune," she said. "You seem even happy!"

The eyes which gazed up at her were softly, wonderfully brilliant. A deeper color crept into the pale cheeks.

"I *am* happy," said the girl, almost in a whisper. "Very, very happy!"

The nurse paused a moment longer, strangely thrilled. Then her training asserted itself.

"You must not excite yourself," she cautioned. "You must go to sleep. Good-night."

"Good-night!" came the murmured answer. "I will try to sleep."

But for long and long she lay staring up into the darkness, glowing with the precious memory of a man's strong arms about her, his ardent lips on hers.

"He is safe," her soul assured her. "He will seek you up and down the world until he finds you.

You shall lie again upon his breast; you shall hear
his heart beating . . . sometime . . . somewhere——"

And with a long sigh of contentment, she closed
her eyes and slept.

THE END

A FEW RECENT PLAYS BY AMERICANS

Beulah M. Dix's ACROSS THE BORDER

A play against war, showing in four scenes, two "beyond the border" of life, the adventures of a highly likable young Lieutenant. He goes on a desperate mission, finds The Place of Quiet and The Dream Girl, as well as The Place of Winds, where he learns the real nature of War, and finally in a field hospital tries to deliver his message. With 2 illustrations. 80 cents net.

New York Tribune: "One of the few pleas for peace that touch both the heart and the intelligence. . . . Its remarkable blending of stark realism with extravagant fancy strikes home. . . . It is well nigh impossible to rid one's mind of its stirring effect."

New York Times: "Impressive, elaborate and ambitious. . . . A voice raised in the theater against the monstrous horror and infamy of war. . . . The Junior Lieutenant has in him just a touch of 'The Brushwood Boy.' "

Of the author's "ALLISON'S LAD" and other one-act plays of various wars ($1.35 net), *The Transcript* said, "The technical mastery of Miss Dix is great, but her spiritual mastery is greater. For this book lives in the memory."

Percival L. Wilde's DAWN and Other One-Act Plays

"Short, sharp and decisive" episodes of contemporary life. Notable for force, interest and at times humor. $1.20 net.

DAWN, a tense episode in the hut of a brutal miner, with a supernatural climax. THE NOBLE LORD, a comedy about a lady, who angled with herself as bait. THE TRAITOR is discovered by a ruse of a British commanding officer. A HOUSE OF CARDS, about a closed door, and what was on the other side—tragic. PLAYING WITH FIRE, a comedy about the devotion of a boy and girl. THE FINGER OF GOD points the way to an ex-criminal by means of a girl he had never seen before.

Lily A. Long's RADISSON: The Voyageur

A highly picturesque play in four acts and in verse. The central figures are Radisson the redoubtable voyageur who explored the Upper Mississippi, his brother-in-law Groseilliers, Owera the daughter of an Indian chief, and various other Indians. The daring resource of the two white men in the face of imminent peril, the pathetic love of Owera, and above all, the vivid pictures of Indian life, the women grinding corn, the council, dances, feasting and famine are notable features, and over it all is a somewhat unusual feeling for the moods of nature which closely follow those of the people involved. $1.00 net.

HENRY HOLT AND COMPANY

PUBLISHERS   NEW YORK

Made in the USA
Las Vegas, NV
27 December 2021

39663336R00177